Also by Robert Sutherland

Mystery at Black Rock Island
The Loon Lake Murders
Son of the Hounds
The Ghost of Ramshaw Castle
Suddenly a Spy
Death Island
If Two Are Dead

THE SECRET OF
DEVIL LAKE

THE SECRET OF
DEVIL LAKE

ROBERT SUTHERLAND

HarperCollins*Publishers*Ltd

http://www.harpercollins.com/canada

First edition

Canadian Cataloguing in Publication Data

Sutherland, Robert, 1925–
    The secret of Devil Lake

ISBN 0-00-648100-0

I. Title.

PS8587.U798S42 1998   jC813'.54   C97-932326-6
PZ7.S97Se 1998

---

98 99 00 ❖ HC 10 9 8 7 6 5 4 3 2 1

Printed and bound in the United States

For Grand and Jean M.
In memory of
"things that go bump in the night"
on Devil Lake

and for Lucille B.,
Westport historian,
with thanks

THE SECRET OF
DEVIL LAKE

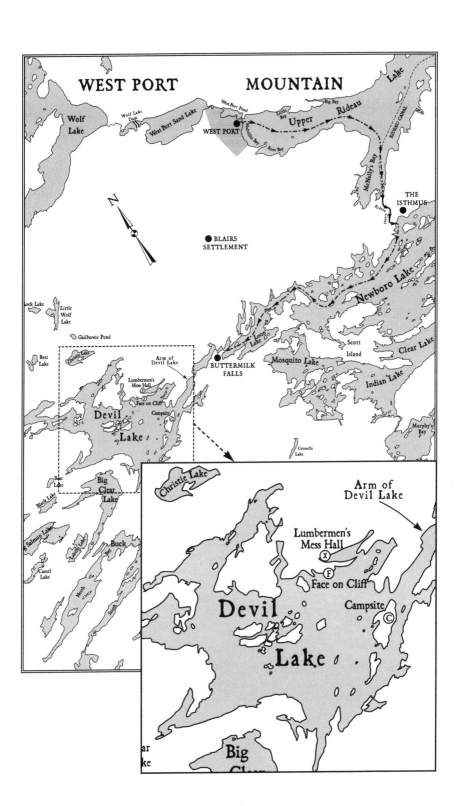

1

"I don't understand you, Will." Sarah was white-faced, her voice on the point of breaking. "How can you run out on us at a time like this?"

"I'm *not* running out!" I pounded my fist on the table in frustration. "Sarah, please! I wouldn't do that. Can't you see—"

"All I see is that when Father and I need you most, you want to go off on some wild scheme of your own and leave us to face . . . to face . . ." She faltered, biting her lip.

"I don't *want* to go, Sarah. You know that. But I . . . I *have* to." How could I make her understand? "I have this feeling. Something tells me—" I stopped. How could I explain this urge to go, to do *something*, anything, rather than sit here and wait for the inevitable? I turned appealingly to the third person in the room, but Reverend Campbell had his back to us and was looking out over the sprawling buildings of Brockville.

"Something tells you," repeated Sarah bitterly. "I suppose you hear voices! Will, Father needs you." Suddenly she reached across the table and caught my hand in hers. "Will," she whispered, "I need you." There were tears in her eyes.

Tears in Sarah's eyes! Tears she had not shed when our little sister succumbed to the ravages of consumption, nor when our dear mother whispered "I love you" for the last time.

Tears she had not shed that day in court when the prosecuting attorney had challenged the jury. I could hear him still . . .

"I ask you to look at the evidence." He pointed an accusing finger at the prisoner in the dock. "This man, Lieutenant James Martin, had opportunity. He was one of the few men who knew that the shipment of money was stored overnight in the blockhouse at the Isthmus. That same money, of course, provided the motive. It is true, as the defence counsel has pointed out, that there were others—a very few others—who had the same opportunity and motive. But only James Martin showed any signs of sudden wealth afterwards—wealth he tried to explain away with some cock-and-bull yarn about an unknown benefactor who most inconveniently died before he could be subpoenaed."

I had looked at the defence lawyer then, hoping to see some sign of confidence. There was none. With a cold, sinking feeling in my gut, I knew he had already conceded defeat. My father was doomed. The prosecuting attorney's closing words burned into my brain forever.

"Gentlemen of the jury, I submit to you that James Martin and an accomplice, Sapper Tom Burgess, stole the aforementioned money, and in carrying out this nefarious deed did commit murder on the person of the commanding officer, Colonel Forrester. Sapper Burgess has already paid with his life at the hands of God for that terrible act. Now it is time that James Martin pay as well. I ask you to bring in the verdict of guilty against James Martin in the theft of the money and the murder of Colonel Forrester."

I had cried all through that mock trial, tears of frustration and anger, as the prosecuting attorney badgered the witnesses and the jury. Although the evidence was circumstantial, in his eyes, and soon in the eyes of the jury, it became clear that only one verdict could be reached.

Even on that last day, Sarah had not cried. She had sat beside me, stoney-faced, remote. Only her hand in mine, clenched so tightly that her nails bit into her own flesh, showed any sign of emotion.

I will never forget that final scene. It will live with me forever.

The jury, filing into the courtroom, trying to appear impassive, avoiding eye contact with the prisoner in the dock. Our father, straight as one of his own ramrods, his face ashen. The judge, eyes piercing beneath black brows, his fingers tap-tapping on the bench . . .

"Gentlemen of the jury, have you reached a verdict?"

"We have, Your Honour. We find the defendant, James Martin, guilty as charged."

Guilty! Strong arms grabbed me. A hand was clamped over my mouth to stifle my cry of protest.

". . . to be taken from this place to the gallows on the morning of the third day of September in the Year of our Lord eighteen hundred and forty-five, and there to be hanged by the neck until you are dead."

No! No! He's innocent! He couldn't do such a thing! But my cries were muffled as I was bundled from the courtroom.

One last glimpse of Father, still proudly erect in his uniform, shrugging free from the court officers, waving to me, calling out something I could not hear.

Then suddenly Sarah was there, brushing past the guards and throwing herself into Father's arms, clinging fiercely to him. One last glimpse of them together before I was dragged away.

Even then Sarah did not cry.

And now I saw tears in her eyes, held back far too long, streaming down her cheeks. And I was the cause.

At that moment I almost gave in. Almost. Then those words came back to me: ". . . to be taken . . . to the gallows . . . the third day of September . . ."

Three weeks! And I had barely a week left. How many of those few precious days had already been lost in idleness? Far too many.

"Sarah," I whispered, clutching her hand, "listen to me. *I can't sit here and do nothing any longer.* If Father didn't steal that money, someone else did. The only way to save Father is to find out who's really guilty."

"And *you* hope to do that?" I winced at the scorn in my older sister's voice. "How? How can *you* find out the truth?"

I was going to say that I didn't know, which would have been the truth, but I caught myself in time. I had to sound confident.

"I'm going up to the Isthmus, where it all happened. Perhaps now that Father has been convicted, the culprit will feel safe and slip up in some way— perhaps spending some of the money." I hesitated. I didn't sound as convincing as I would have liked. "Anyway, I would be doing *something.* And"—I said it again—"I have this feeling that I must go, that something will come of it."

"I see," she said, although her voice suggested otherwise. "And how are you going to explain your 'feeling' to Father? He'll never understand."

"Excuse me." The old minister had turned from the window and was regarding us with compassion

5

in his gentle eyes. "Sarah, dear, I think your father *would* understand Will's feelings. Did he ever tell you about the *Doric*?"

"The *Doric*?" Sarah was mystified. "What's that?"

"A ship," I remembered. "It was lost with all hands. Isn't that right? But what has that got to do with Father?"

"He was supposed to be on that ship, Will. He had his ticket. His luggage was on board. But at the last moment, he had the strongest foreboding—a conviction—that he shouldn't go. He was deliberately late. The *Doric* sailed without him."

"Do you mean to say," wondered Sarah, "that Father is *fey*? That he's a visionary?"

Reverend Campbell shook his head. "I don't think so. No, it was God's hand on his shoulder, holding him back. God had other plans for your father, Sarah. His time hadn't come."

"Other plans! You mean he was saved from drowning so he could die on the gallows? Better if he had gone down with the *Doric*."

"If he had," I said, "we wouldn't be here. That was before we were born."

"I wish we hadn't been born," she said bitterly. "We wouldn't have to face this. And Father would be remembered with honour instead of . . ."

"Don't talk like that," I urged. "Father's still alive. It's not over yet. Something is telling me to go to the Isthmus. I hate to leave you alone, Sarah, but I'm not doing any good sitting around here doing nothing."

Sarah hesitated. I could see she was weakening. Then with a sudden movement she brushed her tears angrily away. She took a deep breath.

"All right," she said, resignedly. "If you must, I won't stop you. But you've got to have a plan. You can't just go with no idea what you're going to do."

"Well," I said, rather lamely, "it happened at the Isthmus, so that's the place to start. The soldiers should still be there. I can ask them what happened . . ."

"Not as Will Martin, you can't. No one will talk to you if they know you're related to Father. You know what it's like around here. We're shunned like the plague. You'll have to pick another name—and you'll have to have a good reason for asking questions."

"Then I will be John Williams." That's my name, John William Martin, though I've been called Will by my family as far back as I can remember. "And I'll say I'm from a newspaper—the Brockville paper. Would that work?"

She considered. "Maybe. You're only fourteen but you can say you're not happy running errands. You want to impress the editor by looking for a new slant on the robbery. Do you think you can do that?"

That sounded easy enough. "Of course I can. That will give me a good excuse to ask questions. Thank you, Sarah. Have you any other ideas?"

"Just that you should talk to Father again if that can be arranged. He might remember details that

could help. But, Will." She caught my hands.
"Don't get his hopes up. Don't make any promises.
And promise *me* one thing. Whatever happens, you
will be back before—" she hesitated, biting her lip,
"—you will be back again to see Father—to say
goodbye."

I gulped. I could only nod, wordlessly. But it was
a promise I must keep at any cost.

2

"Is something wrong?" Father looked at me anxiously as the guard ushered him into the visitors room. "Is it Sarah? They said it was urgent—a family matter."

I didn't answer immediately. I couldn't. I was too appalled at what I saw. We had met with Father several times since his incarceration. He had been washed and shaven then, calm and steady-handed, with words of comfort for both of us. But not this time. There was a three-day growth on his chin and something—was it anxiety or despair?—in his deep-set eyes. And he seemed to have shrunk into the shapeless prison garb. But worst of all was the short chain binding his ankles together. He hobbled across the room, the chain clanking on the floor with every shuffling step.

"Father!" I whispered. "What—?" But then I recovered myself. I couldn't let him see how his appearance affected me. "No," I went on, more steadily, "Sarah's all right. There's no emergency. Perhaps Mr. Campbell had to suggest that to arrange a meeting. I'm sorry if I scared you." My eyes went again to those chains on his ankles. I couldn't help myself. "Do you have to wear those all the time?"

"No, no, lad, don't fret about that." He was recovering his composure. "Not in my cell or in the yard where there are lots of guards. Only if we have to go somewhere unsupervised. They have to be careful. I suppose they searched you? And locked the door behind you? I thought so. Never mind. We're alone for a few minutes." He shuffled across to a low partition that separated us and sat down opposite me. He was able to reach out and clasp my hand tightly in his. "Now, Will, what's this all about?"

I hesitated, not sure how to begin. Suddenly my desire to leave him and Sarah seemed very selfish.

"Papa," I said, using the old endearment we had dropped as we grew older, "do you remember when you were supposed to go to sea on the *Doric*—but didn't? And the ship went down?"

"Of course. One doesn't forget something like that. But why do you ask, Will?"

"Why didn't you go? It's important to me."

He looked surprised, but he answered simply.

"I had a conviction that I shouldn't go. I can't explain it, and I don't expect anyone to understand who hasn't experienced the same thing."

"That's just it," I said eagerly. "The same thing is happening to me. I have this urge to go to the Isthmus. I don't know what I can do when I get there, and I don't want to leave you and Sarah, yet I feel I must. I have this—this conviction that I can do something. Something that will prove your innocence. I have to go to the Isthmus, Papa. That's where it happened. That's where the answer is."

"I see. Yes, I understand. But Sarah—does she understand?"

"Not at first. She cried when I tried to explain."

"She cried? I'm glad to hear that, Will. You and I, we both cried, but not Sarah. She bottled everything up and that's not good. Crying eases pain. I was worried about her. But she shouldn't be left alone."

"She won't be. Mrs. Campbell will be with her, either at home or at the Campbells'."

"In that case," said Father, relieved, "you should go. I don't know whether it's God's hand on you, or whether you simply can't stand to be idle any longer. In either case you have my blessing. But I want to see you again before I—before I die, laddie. I want one last meeting with you and Sarah before I go. We need to strengthen each other. You and Sarah have the hard part."

"*We* do? How can you say that?"

"I'm not afraid to die. Death is merely a doorway into a new and better life. I don't want to go with a rope around my neck. That scares me. But at the end will be a glorious reunion with your sister and your mother and our Lord. But you and Sarah, you have to go on living with the shame."

"You're not going to die," I said fiercely, unreasonably. "If there's a God who saved you once, He'll do it again, or I'll have nothing to do with Him."

"Hold on, son. Don't talk that way. I've had my doubts, God knows, but at the end we have to accept his judgment. As I said, you have the hard part." He looked away, but not before I saw tears in his eyes. For a moment he said nothing. We just clung to each other, hand in hand, across the partition.

"Now, Will," he said at last, smiling. "You're going to the Isthmus. They call it Newboro now. What then? Have you any plans?"

"No," I admitted. "But I'm hoping the real murderer will slip up somehow, now that he's safe. Can you help me, Father? Have you any idea who might have done it?"

He shook his head. "There are several possibilities. Only a few knew the money was to be in the blockhouse overnight, so one of them must have been involved. He either took part or told someone else."

"Who were the few?"

"Well, there was Major Hammond, second in command to the colonel. But apparently he has an alibi. He spent the night at the home of a civilian engineer in West Port—who, by the way, was also one of the few who knew about the money. I forget his name. He was introduced to me by the doctor, another civilian. And I suppose the doctor might have known about it too, come to think of it. He was in to see the colonel that day. The other officers were Lieutenants Blake and Merriton. The three of us were in our quarters all night—separate rooms. None of us has an alibi. Either one of them had as much opportunity and motive as I had."

"So why did they pick on you, Father? Because of that cursed money you were given?"

He sighed wearily. "Mainly that. You help someone and it comes back to haunt you." For just a moment there was bitterness in his voice. He mastered it with an effort. "You know the story, Will. I helped a man who was down and out. I didn't even know his name—I didn't want to know it. But he never forgot. He struck it rich somehow and repaid us a hundredfold. I guess he knew he was going to die and had no relatives. The money came just at the time of the robbery." He shook his head at the irony of it. "My lawyer tried to trace him, but it was too late. The man had died. And, as you know, the jury didn't believe our story."

"I know. I heard it all at the trial. But I want to hear it all again. There may be something I missed—*something* that would help me. Can you tell me exactly what happened the night of the robbery?"

"For me, nothing. I slept all night. But I woke to a great hullabaloo. The theft and murder had been discovered. Someone had broken into the block-house—no mean feat that, I can tell you—and made off with the money. But they had bad luck. The colonel surprised them. They killed him with a fire iron and got away.

"Three days later, after a bad storm, a man was found washed up on the shores of Loon Lake, over near Buttermilk Falls. He had some of the money on him—money that was part of the stolen money. He was a sapper by the name of Tom Burgess, who had been missing since the robbery. And that was another link with me."

"How do you mean?"

"All the other officers had bought their commis-sions. As you know, Will, I came up through the ranks." He spoke with justifiable pride. "And Tom Burgess was in my squad when I was still a sergeant. I spoke to him whenever we met—as I did with all the men from that squad."

"Is that all? How could they hold that against you?" I shook my head in disbelief. "But is there anything else—anything at all—you can tell me?"

He shook his head slowly, reluctantly. "I'm sorry. I wish I could help more but, as I said, I slept through it all. How do you prove that? Every-thing I've said is common knowledge." Then a slight smile touched the corners of his lips. "I guess the colonel wasn't the only surprise the rob-bers got. There was actually a witness who could clear me. If he could be found. And if he could be made to talk."

"Papa," I cried, amazed. "You never said . . . Does the lawyer know . . . ? Who is it?"

"Hold on," he said quickly. "I'm sorry. I shouldn't have given you false hope. You see, the witness is just a bird. A parrot."

A parrot! My hopes plummeted. "What parrot?" I mumbled. I wasn't much interested.

"Colonel Forrester had a pet parrot. Auld Clootie, he called it. Old Devil. A beautiful bird. Often repeated everything you said, clear as a bell. The bird was in the blockhouse that night and I guess its cage was uncovered. In the morning the Colonel was dead, and the money was gone. So was the parrot."

"You mean it flew away? Was the cage door open?"

"No, I mean cage and all were gone. The robbers must have taken it. That's the only explanation. Tom Burgess's canoe was found with the cage still in it. The door was open this time. The bird had flown."

"But—you don't think they took the parrot *because* it was a witness, do you? Maybe it was valuable. Was it?"

"No, not particularly. I can think of only one reason why they took Auld Clootie. The parrot knew too much."

"A *bird* knew too much? You must be joking."

"No, I'm not. Think about it. Two men have broken into the blockhouse. While one is standing guard, the other is getting the money chest out of the cupboard. Suddenly they hear footsteps coming. They try to hide in the darkness. The colonel comes in. They jump him, hit him on the head, probably harder than they intended. The blow kills him. Now they have to work in a hurry. They whisper together in panic, perhaps calling each other by name. The officer decides to stay behind so no one will suspect him. The other will take off with the money and hide it until the hue and cry has died down. Perhaps they even mention the hiding place. They are about to leave. Suddenly a voice speaks up out of the darkness. A voice *repeating everything they have said*. The parrot!

"When they recover from their fright, they have to decide what to do. Kill the bird right there? That might not be so easy. It might make a lot of noise. No, the easiest thing to do is to cover the cage. Parrots are usually quiet when their cage is covered. So they take the cage too, and put it and the chest into the canoe. Burgess takes off across Mud Lake while the officer goes back to bed. Then some time later, I suppose, Burgess kills the bird. Too bad. It was a gorgeous parrot. But it must have given the robbers quite a fright, if events really happened that way."

"Papa, did you tell the lawyer about him? No one said anything about a parrot at the trial."

"Oh, I told him. But he laughed. And that's what the judge and jury would have done too—laugh—if we had brought a bird into court. And it was gone anyway, so it made no difference."

I sighed. None of this helped. Auld Clootie was a

witness, but was probably long dead by now. "Can you think of anything else, Father? Anything at all? The two officers, Blake and Merriton—would they still be in Newboro?"

"As far as I know, they're still there. I can't believe either of them was involved—or how anything could be proven against anyone . . ." His voice trailed off. For just a moment I saw a hint of despair in his eyes. He quelled it with a visible effort. "I don't know what else you can find out, Will, but you can't do any harm and it will keep you occupied. That's important."

I nodded. "Yes, Papa . . ."

The door opened behind him and a guard came in. "Time's up, Martin." He spoke quietly but firmly. "Let's go."

"Yes, all right." Father stood up, still holding my hand. "I'll see you again, Will? Before the third?"

"Yes, I promise. No matter what. And Sarah will be here on visitors day. Goodbye, Papa." A whisper was all I could manage as he turned away and hobbled to the door, chain clanking.

3

The *Bytown* eased gently up to the dock, and I had my first glimpse of the area that had figured so prominently in my father's life. As a soldier with the Royal Engineers, he had had a hand in the building of this section of the Rideau Canal, and it had almost cost him his life. I will never forget the day he arrived home in Brockville, a wasted shadow of his former self, ravaged by swamp fever. The disease, the flies, and the miasma that hovered over the fetid swamps had decimated the gangs of workers, military and civilian alike. The dead lay all around us now, in unmarked graves, the terrible price we paid, Father said, to build this defence against anticipated Yankee invasion.

My father had returned here to see the work completed and to witness the opening of the canal. He had been semi-retired then from active service, and because he was still weak he had not been recalled when the rebellion broke out. A man by the name of Mackenzie had led an uprising against the few who ran the country, hoping to give the ordinary people more power. We had heard little about it at home, but the garrisons on the canal had been put on alert. Some Americans, still dreaming of conquering Canada, had sent some raiding parties across the border in support. The canal was important because it was another link between Kingston and Montreal in case the St. Lawrence river was blockaded. The blockhouse here at Newboro was an important outpost on the waterway.

I could see the blockhouse now, up on the hill. But it didn't appear to be garrisoned anymore. The door was open, and there were no soldiers in sight. Perhaps tension across the border had eased to such an extent that Newboro no longer required them. If so, the men I wanted to meet—Father's fellow officers—would no longer be here. I looked around anxiously.

A number of people were on the dock. Some had disembarked from the steamer. Others were waiting to board, but were in no hurry to do so. The ship had to enter the lock to be lifted to the higher level first. One figure stood out.

He wore grey trousers, and a blue jacket and hat that were trimmed with scarlet. A gold crown glittered on his sleeve. He obviously exercised some authority. I went down the gangplank and approached him.

"Excuse me," I said, touching my cap. "Are you the lock master?"

"That's right," he acknowledged, eyeing me up and down. "Can I help you?"

"I was just wondering—is the blockhouse no longer garrisoned?"

He shook his head. "They were disbanded two days ago. The men have gone home. It doesn't look as if they will be needed any longer."

"I see." I tried to conceal my disappointment. "Could you tell me where"—I picked at random a name my father had mentioned—"Lieutenant Merriton lives?"

"No, 'fraid not. But I'm sure Major Hammond could tell you. That's him over there." Then before I had a chance to plan my next move, he called out, "Major Hammond! Young chap here wants to talk to you."

Major Hammond! So this was one of the men my father had mentioned. The one with the alibi. But alibis could sometimes be proven false . . .

He was a red-faced man with a bristling moustache and a very hearty manner. At least, it was hearty at that moment, perhaps because he was in conversation with two women, a young girl about my own age, and a man in clerical garb.

They all looked at me expectantly, so I had to approach them, wondering how to proceed.

"Hello," I said, tipping my cap. "I'm Will Martin."
I could have kicked myself. What would Sarah
say if she had heard me? "You can't use your own
name," she had said. But it was too late now. And
thank heaven Martin is a common name. I was
relieved that they accepted it without comment. I
would have to stick to my real name from now on.
The major made the introductions. "This is Mrs.
Meadows and her daughter Tabitha." The lady,
twirling a pink parasol, was tall and attractive with
stray ringlets of blonde hair escaping around the
brim of a large hat. Her daughter had burnished
copper curls and very dark eyes. At least, I thought
her eyes were dark. I had only a glimpse before
long lashes hid them.

She didn't look anything like Sarah, yet I was
suddenly reminded of my sister. Perhaps it was the
mischievous twinkle I caught in this girl's eye
before it was masked behind a demure lowering of
her lashes. There used to be sparkles in Sarah's
eyes, back before our tragedy.

Suddenly I realized how very much alone I was.
How I longed for a friend to share my burden. I
would never have thought that friend might turn out
to be a girl. Girls were supposed to be—well, timid
and modest. But there were exceptions. Sarah had
once given me a black eye when taking exception
to my teasing, much to my surprise—and approval.
And I would bet this girl—Tabitha—was like that
too. If only . . . But the major was continuing with
the introductions.

21

". . . and Reverend and Mrs. Munro." Reverend Munro extended a long white hand that was surprisingly firm. His wife, who was a little plump and comfortable looking, gave me a welcoming smile. "And I am Major Hammond. You wished to speak to me?"

"I'm sorry to bother you," I apologized. "I just wondered if you could tell me where I could find Lieutenant Merriton."

"Merriton? Sorry, lad. We were disbanded, so it's back to civilian life for all of us. He's going home to Perth. Blake, Merriton, and I all live there. Are you a friend of his?"

But he didn't wait for an answer, so I didn't bother correcting him. "Take the Tay branch in to Perth. That's the way I'm going."

So all three suspects—suspects to me, at least—would be in Perth at the same time! My guardian angel must still be directing me. Yes, I would take the Tay branch into that town. Then I would introduce myself as the reporter Sarah had suggested. I thanked the major and bowed out from the little company.

I watched as the *Bytown* nosed into the lock, the gates closed, and the boat was raised to the new level. Then, along with a number of other passengers, I stepped aboard and she slipped out of the lock into a narrow, winding channel. The forest reached to the water's edge, and here and there granite cliffs soared abruptly from the banks. I could hardly believe that I was on the canal—the canal my father had helped to build. Lost in my thoughts, I jumped a little when a voice spoke.

"Are you travelling alone, Mr. Martin?"

The major's company had come up to join me near the bow. It was Mrs. Meadows who spoke.

"I—yes, I am."

"Then you would be welcome to join our party. We are travelling as far as West Port—except for the major, who will be going on to Perth."

"Thank you. That is very kind. Is it far to West Port?"

"No, it is our next port of call. We will be there by four o'clock."

She looked out at the channel we were entering, and I couldn't help drawing her attention to the canal. "It is a marvellous piece of engineering, isn't it?" I was proud of my father's part in it, but I couldn't mention that.

"Yes." The woman's voice was wistful. "But the cost was high. Terribly high. My first husband— Tabitha's father—died of swamp fever." I wanted to tell her that the same terrible illness had almost killed my own father. But I couldn't let on, in case she connected me with a condemned killer.

"My present husband," she continued, "was more fortunate. He was not affected."

"Was he an army engineer?" If so, I thought, he would know my father.

"An engineer, yes, but a civilian. Since the completion of the canal, he has been working in West Port."

Suddenly I remembered something else my father had said. Major Hammond had spent the fatal night with a civil engineer in West Port. That was his alibi. Could it be . . .?

"I have heard," I said, "that this was the worst part of the entire canal to build, because of the rock and swamp."

"That's right." The minister had joined us. He pointed. "They had to cut a clearing from Mud Lake to the Upper Rideau so that the breeze could get through and clear out the swamp air. Then they cut this channel through by hand. A lot of men died here. Their graves—most of them unmarked—are all around us."

Thanks to their sacrifice, I knew, we were winding our way along a meandering watercourse, lined by verdant trees. A gentle breeze ruffled the leaves and the sweet song of many birds came to us from the surrounding forest.

"People like my father sacrificed their lives." Tabitha had come up beside me, her hand almost touching mine on the rail. Her eyes met mine, friendly, not shy as they were supposed to be. "Have you been this way before, Mr. Martin?"

Mr. Martin! I wanted her to call me Will, but I didn't think her mother would approve. I shook my head.

"No . . ." I didn't know what to say. *I* was the shy one. I was both relieved and disappointed when her mother interrupted.

Mrs. Meadows was looking overhead where grey

clouds were gathering. "I fear it is about to rain, and this parasol is meant to keep the sun off, not rain. We had better go below."

"A little rain won't hurt us, Mama," protested Tabitha.

"Maybe not," agreed her mother, patiently, "but it won't do that frock any good. Would you like to come with us, Mr. Martin? Come, Tabby."

Tabby! What a nickname! It made her sound like a cat. I was startled to note that her eyes, meeting mine, were not as dark as I had thought. In the fading sunlight they were positively green, just like a cat's—for only a moment, then they vanished again behind those long lashes.

"I think we had better all go below," said the major, taking charge. "The rain probably won't last long, but I expect it will be heavy while it does."

As drops began to fall, Mrs. Meadows and Tabitha hurried over to the steps that led below deck, followed by the major and the Munros. I gathered my belongings and headed down the stairs with them. Suddenly, we all froze.

An inhuman cry ripped apart the pleasant stillness of the afternoon.

4

My blood ran cold.

I know that's a trite phrase, but I can think of no other words that come close to expressing my reaction to the terrible sound.

In stunned silence we stood staring at each other, while shivers crawled like spiders up my spine. In the hushed silence, the chuff-chuff of the steam engine was startingly loud and clear.

We looked around at each other, well aware that none of us had uttered a sound. Yet someone had screamed, that was certain. Where, then, had the scream come from?

The sound of feet on the gangway from the deck above awoke us as if from a trance. The ship's captain appeared, his boots loud on the iron steps. He stopped at the bottom and stared around, wide-eyed, as if expecting to find someone in the throes of death.

"What happened?" he demanded. "Who screamed?"

We all shook our heads, as mystified as the captain.

In those brief moments I looked around at the other members of our little group.

Mrs. Meadows was like a carved statue, white-faced, her hand at her mouth, her eyes wide with horror. Tabitha's eyes—yes, they were green—were wide too, but with surprise and curiosity. She had every right to be afraid, but somehow she wasn't. Again she reminded me of Sarah.

Reverend Munro had half risen, gripping his cane with one white-knuckled hand, clasping his wife's with the other. Mrs. Munro bit her lip, her fine grey eyes troubled, questioning. Beside them the major appeared in shock, only his military moustache aquiver.

We stared stupidly at the captain and could do nothing but shake our heads in bewilderment.

Suddenly it came again—a high, piercing cry that seemed to fill the deck. It stopped abruptly. Then, into our horrified silence, a hollow voice spoke. It was curiously harsh, yet the words were clear.

"Auld Clootie knows the devil's secret." A throaty laugh followed that cryptic remark.

And now we were all staring in one direction. For the voice had come from a pile of luggage at the foot of the gangway.

The captain stepped back sharply against the rail. For a moment he didn't move. Then he reached out a hand slowly, and I could see from where I stood that it trembled. On top of the pile of luggage something—perhaps the size and shape of a human head—was covered with a sheet. He gripped the sheet, hesitated a moment, and then with an indrawn breath yanked it clear.

On top of the pile was a cage, and in that cage a gaudy bird, all green and gold and scarlet, with wicked black eyes. It shook its head, ruffling gorgeous feathers. "Good morning," it said, harsh and clear. "Auld Clootie says good morning."

Auld Clootie! My father's words came back to me in a rush and I stared in disbelief at the iridescent creature. It had to be! There couldn't be two birds with that strange name. Colonel Forrester's parrot was here, inexplicably still alive. Here was a witness that could save my father's life . . .

As if to clinch the matter, the bird turned and looked directly at me, or so it seemed, evil eyes gleaming. "Auld Clootie knows!" it shrilled again. Then it abruptly turned its back on all of us, withdrew its head into a ruff of feathers, and was silent.

There was a gentle luffing sound as all of us released our pent-up breath.

"Well!" Mrs. Meadows was saying, her voice unsteady. "I never heard of such a thing."

"What a magnificent bird," breathed Tabitha.

"Unbelievable," whispered Mrs. Munro.

"Incredible," agreed her husband. "How long has it been there? Strange that it has been silent for so long."

"Not really," rumbled the major. "Strange, rather, that it should speak up now. Birds are usually silent as long as their cage is covered. But did you catch what it said? Auld Clootie. A strange name, you'll agree."

I looked at him sharply. He had to know that this was the colonel's parrot and that it had disappeared the night of the murder. Was he just surprised—or was he alarmed? I wished I had caught his first reaction when the captain had pulled the sheet off the cage, but it was too late now. He simply looked interested.

"The bird was loaded at Seeleys Bay." The captain had found an attached label and was reading it. "To Captain Bowley, West Port." His eyes swept the assembled passengers. "Anyone know him?"

"I do." Reverend Munro inclined his head. "A retired sailor. Has been around the world, and has many a tale to tell—if you can stomach his language. Great old chap. Kind of man you might expect to own a parrot."

"Well, he'll own one when we get to West Port, which won't be long now."

I scarcely heard any of this. I was too shaken, too excited. There was the witness, right there, alive and talking. If only Sarah was there to share my excitement.

I suddenly wondered if my agitation was noticeable and I looked around quickly. No one was paying any attention to me—except Tabitha. She was looking at me with frank curiosity. If only I could share my troubles with her! But I couldn't. No one must know that I was the son of a convicted killer. If she knew that—if anyone knew— I would be shunned like a pariah. I was alone.

I wasn't actually alone, of course, though for the rest of the trip, paradoxically, I wanted to be. I wanted to sort things out, to make plans, but they involved me in their chatter, and if my comments were inane or off-target no one seemed to notice. Except maybe Tabitha, and I tried to avoid her eyes. When the rain shower let up and they went back to the upper deck I didn't want to go. I wanted to stay there and keep an eye on that bird. But I couldn't think of an excuse when they urged me to accompany them.

And when, a short time later, West Port came in sight, nestling at the foot of a hill, I had to make up my mind. Should I go on to Perth, and start asking questions? Or should I keep an eye on that parrot? Was I being absurd to hope that a bird might help me? Would I be wasting precious time when I could be questioning people who had been involved?

Major Hammond decided for me.

"Mrs. Meadows," he called, "I must have a word with your husband. Just a moment and I will come with you." He turned to the ship's captain. "If I'm not back on board when you're ready to sail, go on without me."

Had his change of plans anything to do with the parrot? I couldn't be sure, but the major's words helped me make up my mind. I picked up my bag.

A strange feeling of foreboding came over me as I started down the gangplank.

5

West Port harbour was bustling. I knew, from my father's reminiscences, that many of the stone-masons employed in the building of the canal had settled here, especially the Irish. Some farmed, wresting a living from the topsoil that barely covered bedrock. Other were millers or lumbermen, or tradesmen catering to their own countrymen. And the canal boats were their link to the outside world.

This one slipped her moorings and chuffed off in the direction of the Narrows Lock. Only the deck master and I were left on the wharf, standing beside the covered cage.

All this time not a sound came from the parrot, still hidden by the sheet, though the cage had been moved more than once when it proved to be in someone's way. Mr. Bowley had not come to claim his package.

The harbour master took a ponderous watch from his pocket, glanced from it to the sun as if to check one with the other, replaced it, looked curiously at me, and then stared pointedly at the covered cage.

"We seem to have one unclaimed piece of cargo, Mr. . . .?"

"Martin," I said. "Will Martin."

"Mr. Martin. And I don't see any address tag either."

"There's one under the sheet," I said. "It's a birdcage with a parrot in it. It caused quite a stir on board when it screamed and then started to talk. I've been wondering who owns it. I would like to talk to him. You see, I'm interested in parrots." One, in particular.

"Is that a fact," murmured the man. He lifted the sheet, eyed the bird for a moment, then turned the tag to read it. The bird raised its head from deep in its ruff and muttered sulkily, "Wring their filthy necks," then retracted its head again.

The startled harbour master stepped back and glanced at me. "Did you hear that? It talks, all right. Better watch what it's saying or someone will wring *its* filthy neck."

"Watch what it's saying," repeated the bird. "Wring its filthy neck." Auld Clootie swung its head, still low in the ruff, and gave me an evil glare. It laughed, then said harshly, "Auld Clootie knows."

The harbour master laughed, just a little tremulously. "Fancy that! Never heard a bird talk so plain before. And this is for Stephen Bowley, eh? Now what in the world does he want with a talking feather duster?" He turned and looked up the road. "No sign of him. If he thinks I'm going to deliver a bird that talks bloody murder . . ."

Suddenly I had an idea. This was too good an opportunity to lose. "Perhaps I can help," I offered hurriedly. "If you can tell me where Mr. Bowley lives, I don't mind delivering the parrot myself."

"You?" He eyed me thoughtfully. He didn't know me, but I was a solution to a problem. And I wasn't likely to walk off into the bush with a "talking feather duster." It didn't take him long to make up his mind.

"You'll not have far to go. Straight up this road to the end and turn right. First house past the cemetery. You can't miss it. And if you want to leave your bag here meantime, it will be safe enough with me. I'm here till six o'clock."

"All right, I'll do that. This Mr. Bowley—what's he like?"

"A retired sea captain. And if you want my opinion, I wouldn't be surprised but what he was one of them pirates. Has more money than an honest seaman has any right to, anyhow.

"Drinks it away. A fine man when he's sober, which ain't often. You might find him sleeping it off with fumes thick in the house. If so, just leave the bird. Reckon he'll come round and feed it sooner or later."

"Very well. I'm off."

I removed the sheet so that I could carry the cage by the ring on top, folded the sheet under my arm, and started out with my strange cargo.

At first the bird said nothing, merely opening its eyes to see what was going on and then closing them, withdrawing its head. I was glad of the silence. We were causing enough of a stir as it was. A complete stranger walking the streets of the village, carrying a gaudy bird that even in silence told of faraway tropical lands, was not a common sight. I met the inquisitive looks I encountered on the way with a smile and a nod, and received the same in return.

What would this Mr. Bowley be like? Why was the parrot being sent to him? Would *he* know anything that would be of help? I certainly hoped so. Otherwise I was wasting precious time. I had an uneasy feeling that was exactly what I was doing. And yet— this creature, bird or not, was the only witness.

There was no one in sight when I turned past the cemetery, though I spied one dirty, freckled face watching me from the last corner. So I couldn't be sure whether anyone saw me walk up to the log cabin with its crooked door.

The place was in silence. Not even a dog barked, though plenty had heralded my approach through the village. I knocked loudly on the door, but received no response. A bit nervously, I went around the back of the log cabin. Here was an open doorway into a lean-to shed piled high with chopped wood. An inner door was ajar.

I knocked again, then pushed my way in. I found myself in a kitchen, with a blackened stove on which sat a pot brimming with some unknown, scum-covered contents. On a table set for one, I saw a chipped pot of cold coffee, an open jar of jam surrounded by buzzing flies, and a piece of hard bread. But of Mr. Bowley there was no sign. Perhaps, as the harbour master had suggested, he was somewhere sleeping it off.

The bird chose this moment to speak. "Devil's face," it said sleepily. "Watch for the devil's face." Then, incredibly, it started to sing. "Trust in the Lord and don't despair!" Just as abruptly, it stopped and laughed. "Thou shalt not kill," it then announced. "Auld Clootie knows."

"I hope you know a lot," I muttered. "In fact, I'm counting on it. I just wonder if Mr. Bowley knows anything—if I can find him."

I opened an inner door, and had my answer—though not, at first, the correct one. He hadn't made it to the bed, which was against the wall, covers awry. He lay on the floor, arms and legs flung wide. To my surprise, I could smell no alcohol fumes, although the open window might account for that. I stepped closer for a better look at the bearded face—and stopped cold, my heart pounding suddenly, suffocatingly.

"No," said the parrot, suddenly alert. "Down with the Tories! Look for the devil's face!" I paid no attention. I was staring, thunderstruck, at the haft of a knife buried deep in Mr. Bowley's chest, and the dried blood that stained his nightshirt.

6

Somehow I got myself outside and leaned weakly against the door post, taking in deep draughts of cool air.

"Hey, mister, where's that bird you was carrying?"

I jumped at the sudden appearance of a freckled face bobbing up from behind a tombstone. I looked down at my shaking hand where, last I remembered, the cage had been. It wasn't there. I supposed I must have set it down inside.

"Never mind that," I said, my voice cracking. "Is there a doctor in town?" Not that a doctor would do any good now. "Or a constable?"

A sudden heart-stopping shriek burst from the house behind me. After a moment of petrified silence, a throaty voice shouted, "Down with the government! Up with Mackenzie! Auld Clootie knows!"

The freckled face was fast disappearing down the road, propelled by a furiously working pair of legs. I let him go. I seemed to be paralysed by the horror of what I had found. I don't know what I would have done then if someone else hadn't appeared on the scene.

A lad of my own age was approaching. He wore a cloth cap, suspenders, and knee breeches. He tried to stop the fleeing urchin without success, then saw me and ran towards the cabin.

"What was that racket?" he asked. Then he paused. "You're the chap who was carrying the bird—the parrot. Right?"

"That's right. I'm Will Martin. And didn't I see you meet the minister at the dock?"

"Yep. I'm Tod Munro. Are you all right? You look ill."

"*I'm* all right, but Mr. Bowley isn't. Is there a doctor in town?"

"Sure. Doctor Farr. Down by the pond, but it'll take a few minutes to get him. Maybe my mother could help. She's done some nursing and we live just down the road."

I shook my head. "He's past that. Fact is, he's past doctoring too. What we really need is an undertaker. And a constable."

"An undertaker? He's *dead*?"

"Not only dead. Murdered."

39

"M-murdered?" Tod's face had turned ashen, but there was excitement in his eyes. "How?"

"A knife. In the chest. He's dead. No doubt about it."

"Golly!" he breathed. "A murder! In West Port! You're not joking? No, I can see you're not. There *is* a constable but—look, I'll get my pa. He'll know what to do." He stopped short as a harsh laugh echoed through the log cabin. "What *is* that racket? The bird? What's it doing here in West Port, anyhow?"

"I'll explain later," I promised. "Right now, it might be better if you get your father."

"Right. You better sit down while I'm gone."

He ran off and I took his advice and sat down on the grass. I wasn't going back in that house, bird or no bird, until I had to.

The minister arrived first. He knew me, of course.

"Mr. Martin! This is terrible, what Tod's been telling me. I sent for the doctor and the law. I'll just go in and take a look."

I nodded and stayed where I was until he came out. His white face told me that any doubts he may have had about my story were gone.

"He's dead, of course. Probably has been for some time. The doctor might be able to say for how long. Poor Walker! He'll be out of his depth."

"Walker?"

"He represents the law around here. Good at arresting drunks—he's well acquainted with Mr. Bowley, I assure you—and chasing boys, but he's

never had to deal with anything like this before."
Reverend Munro looked at me sharply. "I don't
understand how you happen to be here. Last I knew
you were on the steamer bound for Perth."

"I changed my mind," I explained. "West Port
looked like such a beautiful place that I decided at
the last moment to stay over. Then the parrot was
left on the dock and the man in charge didn't know
what to do with it, so I offered to deliver it, and"—I
jerked my thumb over my shoulder—"that's what I
found."

"I see. Well, the poor thing's without an owner
now. I wonder what will become of it."

I hadn't had time to think about that. But suddenly
the parrot's future was very important indeed. I had
good reason to want to keep it alive . . .

"Has he any relatives—Mr. Bowley, I mean?"

The minister hesitated, then shook his head
uncertainly. "Not that I know of. Not around here
anyway. Poor chap. What on earth could have happened? Why would anyone want to kill him? It
doesn't make sense."

"Robbery, maybe?"

"Rob old Bowley? I suppose it's possible. He
seemed to have lots of money for drink, and rumour
had it that he kept it hidden in the house. Maybe
someone believed that. But no, you can't tell me
that anyone around here would kill him for his
money."

"Perhaps it was supposed to be just a robbery,
and Mr. Bowley caught the thief in the act."

He shook his head unhappily. "I suppose it's possible," he admitted again. "But *who*? People in West Port don't kill. There may be some tempted to steal—I'm sure there are. We're all human. But *kill*? No! West Port people don't kill! I wonder if there was a struggle. Did you notice anything?"

I shook my head dumbly.

"It would be hard to tell in that house anyway. No, it must have been a stranger." He stopped again and looked at me. "And *you're* a stranger . . ."

I jumped up, startled and flushed. "Hey, wait a minute. I just arrived in West Port. You know that. And he's been dead some time. You said so yourself."

He laid a hand on my shoulder. "I know that. And it's just as well I do. Because the townspeople will be looking for a stranger, and you're on the scene. Some people jump to conclusions and believe only the facts that support their theories." How well I knew the truth of that! But Reverend Munro continued. "How long will you be staying around? And where?"

"At the hotel. At least—I suppose there is one?"

"Oh yes. I suggest the Stage Coach Inn. How long did you intend to stay?"

"I hadn't thought about it, but not for too long. I hope I won't be detained because of . . ." I jerked my thumb in the direction of the cabin again.

"You might be, but probably not for long. I can vouch for the fact that you were on the *Bytown* with me and with Major Hammond. He carries more weight around here than I do. But they'll want to hear what you have to say, I expect, and where you can be reached if it ever comes to a trial. But this will all take time. Walker will turn it over to the authorities in Brockville, I expect. Well, that's up to him, thank God."

Doctor Farr arrived at that moment. He came astride a chestnut gelding, and was out of the saddle while dust still whirled about the horse's hooves. He was a big man, not tall, but powerful and efficient.

"Archie!" He greeted the minister warmly. "Just back from the O'Gradys'. Their sixth. Another girl. Mother and daughter doing well. Father doubtful. Now then, what's this all about? Tod had some wild tale about old Bowley being dead."

"He's right," said Mr. Munro seriously. "With a knife sticking in his chest."

"What! You must be—no, you wouldn't joke about something like that. So Tod meant it when he said he was going for Walker." His eye fell on me and I could see his reaction. A murder, and here was a stranger at the scene. "Who's this?"

"This is Will Martin, Doctor Farr. Will discovered the body when he kindly delivered a package for Ed Murphy down at the dock."

"Ah." The doctor looked at me speculatively for a moment, then turned. "I'll take a look. Lead the way, Archie."

The minister agreed reluctantly and they left me alone, which was fine with me. I needed time to think, to try to sort things out in my mind. I had many questions to ask myself.

I dismissed the first question at once. Had this murder anything to do with the parrot? Not likely— I couldn't see how. The second question was more difficult. Was there some connection between the parrot and the source of Mr. Bowley's money? In other words, could the dead man have been involved in the robbery at the blockhouse? Again, I couldn't see how, but anything was possible, as Father was fond of saying . . .The third question was the important one. Since I wasn't going to get any answers out of a dead man, I was left with the daunting task of questioning a parrot. How was I to go about that—if, indeed, I ever had the opportunity?

Constable Walker arrived then, accompanied by Tod Munro. The constable wasn't as big as the doctor and wore no uniform or badge, but he managed to look important anyway.

"You'll be Will Martin, who discovered the body. Tod told me about you. Martin, eh? Any relation to the man who robbed the blockhouse and murdered the colonel?"

I hesitated only a moment, fighting down a feeling of panic. "No," I said shortly.

"It's a common name," he admitted. "You two wait right here. Is the doctor inside?"

At my nod he went into the house, leaving Tod and me alone. Tod was looking at me with something like envious awe.

"Imagine finding a dead man! It must have been horrible. Think they'd let me go in and look?"

I shook my head. "You wouldn't want to—" I broke off as a sudden, now familiar shriek rang out from inside the cabin. After the inevitable moment of startled silence, the hoarse voice proclaimed, "This is the day that the Lord hath made. We will rejoice and be glad in it." The harsh laugh followed, then a subdued, but distinct, "Wring his filthy neck."

Tod and I stared at each other. We pictured the three men inside the cabin suddenly shocked out of their wits. And we both began to laugh, a little hysterically.

The reappearance of the solemn-faced men stopped us cold.

"He's been dead since the early morning hours," said the doctor.

"That lets you off the hook, young man." The constable was obviously disappointed. "Reverend Munro claims that you were with him on the boat. Still, I want to know more about you. I'll have to call in the authorities and they will want to talk to you. You will have to stay around."

I nodded. A trip to Perth was out of the question for now at least, but as long as the parrot was nearby, a day or two in West Port might not be time wasted. "I'll stay at an inn, I guess. Probably the Stage Coach." Since they knew I couldn't be guilty, I wasn't too worried about the "authorities." But there was one thing I was worried about. "What about the parrot? What happens to it?"

"The bird has already made a fine suggestion," growled the constable. "'Wring his filthy neck.' Seems like a good idea to me."

I hoped he wasn't serious. "Mr. Bowley may have distant relatives," I suggested, rather vaguely. "If not, I'd like to keep the parrot myself, if there's no objection."

"If there *are* relatives," said the doctor, "it's going to take some time to locate them, so someone's going to have to take the bird. As far as I'm concerned it might as well be you. But if so, you won't be staying at the Stage Coach. They wouldn't tolerate such a racket."

I hadn't thought of that, but he was probably right. What was I to do? I *had* to have some time alone with the parrot. It was Tod who came to my rescue.

"Couldn't we keep it if no one claims it, pa? The bird, I mean. Out in the barn. They're quiet when the cage is covered, aren't they?"

That's not necessarily the case with this bird, I thought, but I didn't say so. "Perhaps if the parrot stays with you, it'll only sing hymns and quote the Bible," I suggested, and was dangerously close to another hysterical giggle. "It seems to know a bit of both."

"Well, we can't wring the bird's neck," agreed the minister. "All right, if you're agreeable, Walker, we'll take the parrot on trial for a day or two. And you, lad, never mind the hotel. Come and stay with us until the law has finished with you, and then you can be on your way. Maybe by then we'll know what to do with the bird."

I was surprised and delighted at the generous offer. "Thank you very much, Mr. Munro. I don't want to impose—"

"You won't be imposing," broke in Tod, apparently as pleased as I was. "Mother likes to have company."

"Listen," snapped Constable Walker impatiently, "it don't matter to me what you do with that creature. Just get it out of the house so I can do my job in peace. A man's been murdered. Everyone clear out and let me be. Go get the bird if you want it, but don't touch anything. Then skedaddle. Just don't leave West Port, Mr. Martin."

I went back into the house. I hadn't remembered leaving the cage on the stove, but that's where I found it. I picked it up, and kept my eyes away from the room where the body lay. The parrot's head was high out of the ruff. Black eyes looked at me. "Auld Clootie knows," it said. Mockingly, it seemed to me.

"I *know* you know," I muttered. "But are you going to tell? That's the question." I leaned over to pick up the cage's cover, which had fallen to the floor. As I did so, I saw a piece of paper lying beneath the sheet. I picked that up too, unthinking, and set it on the table. A glance showed me that it was a letter and that the heading read, in neat handwriting, "Kingston," with the date of ten days ago. Something more than ill-mannered curiosity prompted me to cast my eyes over the body of the letter, and one word seemed to stand out from the rest. "Parrot," it said. I didn't take time to read any more.

"Don't touch anything," the constable had said. Undeterred, I shoved the letter into my pocket, a little guiltily.

Anything to do with the parrot could be of the utmost importance.

7

Why had the robbers not killed the parrot, silenced it forever, as my father had supposed? Who had sent it to Captain Bowley—and why? I hoped the letter buried deep in my pocket would answer these questions, but I didn't have a chance to find out for several hours.

Tod and I settled the parrot in the barn, which it was to share with a cow and horse. They were both stolid creatures, unlikely to be disturbed by anything short of an earthquake. I was shown into a comfortable room with a feather bed, a wash basin and jug in a wild rose pattern, and a matching receptacle under the bed. But with no time alone, I had no chance then to so much as glance at the letter.

*　　*　　*

I was invited to join the family for supper. The Munros were so warm and friendly that a wave of homesickness threatened to overwhelm me. What was Father doing now? How was he acting when there was no one to encourage, no one from whom he had to hide his real feelings? Was he afraid? Was he bitter? And how was Sarah putting in the long, anxious hours? Was I selfish in thinking that only *I* must have something to occupy my mind during these days of waiting for the end? The Munros respected my reticence, putting it down, no doubt, to shock at my grisly discovery. Tod was anxious to talk about Captain Bowley's death, but his parents discouraged him. It would be a relief to share my burden, and I was beginning to think that Tod would be the friend in need I had wished for.

After supper Tod and I went to the barn to feed the parrot. We tried some oats from the horse's stall, but the bird refused them, clearly insulted, so we gave it some sunflower seeds. Auld Clootie accepted them without enthusiasm. It had only one remark to make before the cage was covered.

"The devil's face," it said. "Look for the devil's face."

Tod and I looked at each other and shrugged. The devil's face? It seemed to me the devil's face was right there, surrounded by gorgeous feathers.

"The bird don't make much sense, does it," remarked Tod.

"Sometimes it does." I resisted the impulse to tell him everything then and there. No, I wanted to read that letter first. "I'm going to bed now, Tod. But in the morning we've got to talk."

"Talk?" Tod was mystified. "Talk about what?"

"I'll tell you then. Good night, Tod."

For a long moment I held the letter in my hand unopened. Could it possibly lead to proof of my father's innocence? No, that was asking too much. I musn't think like that. Disappointment would be too much to bear. I opened it.

"Dear Captain Bowley," I read at last. "You don't know me, but it is only due to your bravery and expert seamanship at the time of the sinking of the *Heloise* that I and a number of other passengers are alive today."

I stopped reading for a moment. I had a momentary vision of a ship in distress amid mountainous waves, with the sails gone and the rigging down, and the passengers waiting in terror for a watery grave. But the captain, cool and calm in command, somehow brings them safely through. That man lying on a lonely cabin floor with a knife in his chest had a gallant past.

"I know," continued the letter, "that during the disaster you lost your pet parrot, of which you were very fond. I remembered your loss when I had to decide what to do with my own bird.

"I am about to go into hospital, and will not come out except to be buried. I therefore must make provision for my parrot. I am going to ship it to you on the *Bytown* as a token of my gratitude and as a means of providing for its future.

"It may be, of course, that you no longer want, or are in a position to care for, a parrot. In that case you are at liberty to sell it. I have had a gentleman on my doorstep several times who is anxious to purchase it, offering a ridiculously large sum for it. In my present straits money no longer interests me, but I hope that either the bird or the money it can bring will be of interest to you, and in some small way repay the debt I owe.

"I have told the gentleman what I intend to do with the parrot, and no doubt he will call on you with the same tempting offer. His name is Smith.

"The bird's name is Auld Clootie, which I take to mean Old Devil, given it by one of its former owners. By its talk I deduce that it probably had several of these, at least one of a violent nature and one who supported Mackenzie in the recent rebellion. The hymns and Bible verses the bird learned from me, but I regret they are vastly outnumbered by strange references to the devil. I have had little time to work with the parrot. I found it flying loose quite some time ago, just after the big storm, and failed to trace its owners.

"You saved my life many years ago, but I have never forgotten, and took the trouble to find out that you have retired to a village not so far from my present home in Seeleys Bay. As my life draws to a close and I commit my soul to God, I do this small thing in the hope that it will bring you some measure of contentment one way or another." The letter was signed "Nathaniel Hope."

I blew out my lamp and pulled the covers up to my chin, but it was a long time before I fell asleep. I was thinking of a gallant captain, brought low by drink, dying on the floor of a log cabin with a knife in his chest; of a grateful man concerned about the welfare of a parrot, and remindful of the man who had once saved his life. But more than anything I was thinking of Auld Clootie. Nathaniel Hope had found it flying loose "just after the big storm." Oh yes, this was the bird all right. This was the witness to the murder for which my father was to pay with his life.

And I was thinking of an unknown man named Smith who, for some reason, was desperately anxious to get hold of the parrot that was now in my possession.

I was not so sure anymore that the letter had nothing to do with the murder of Captain Bowley.

8

Sometime through the night I was awakened. One moment I was asleep, the next wide awake, every sense alert. In spite of the pitch darkness I knew where I was. And I knew that some sound had awakened me—some sound from outside.

I was in a strange house, in a strange village, with no idea which sounds might be strange and which might be normal. Yet something propelled me out of bed and over to the window. Any light from the sky was blanketed behind heavy clouds, so I could distinguish little at first except shadows. Then I saw a dark figure detach itself momentarily from the gloom below, cross the open space, and merge with the black bulk of the barn. I heard the creaking of hinges, then silence.

Mr. Munro, I told myself, or Tod, checking the animals. But I didn't really believe that. This person was furtive, obviously with criminal intent—and the parrot that might possibly save my father's life was in that barn.

I pulled on my pants, shirt, and shoes and opened the bedroom door. The house was in total darkness. I felt my way gingerly to the stairs and down, hanging onto the rail. The steps creaked alarmingly, but no one seemed to hear me. I found the front door, eased it open, and slipped outside.

The night was warm and still. Somewhere an owl hooted mournfully, accentuating the deep silence all round.

I crossed the yard to the barn. The door was open. For a moment I stood, undecided. Should I call for help? No, I would have to explain everything then, and there was no time for that. I was scared. But I *had* to find out what was going on. I felt my way inside, my eyes trying to pierce the gloom. In the inner stall, the horse moved, its heavy feet thudding on the plank floor; then it was still.

Suddenly to my right a light flickered. A momentary flare, then a steady glow. Someone had lit a lantern. I could see him, a dark, bulky figure, grotesquely large in the distorting light from the lantern. He held the light high, looking around, his back to me. I shrank into the shadows.

The light fell on the covered cage.

The man set the light down, hesitated, then slowly lifted the sheet. Auld Clootie stirred, head moving in its ruff. One eye opened, reflecting the light of the lantern.

The man whispered softly, soothingly. He raised a gloved hand slowly, smoothly, and opened the cage door. The parrot watched as if mesmerized, its eyes following the hand that reached in for it. Then it hopped down, still without a sound, and perched on the man's hand.

"Good boy, steady now." The man spoke in a hoarse whisper. He stepped back, arm extended.

Flat against the wall I groped around, hoping to find something that would serve as a weapon. My hand closed on a long, slender piece of wood. A rake or fork handle, I guessed. Too awkward, whatever it was. I needed something shorter, heavier . . .

He was coming, slowly, the bird on one hand, the lantern in the other. He stopped then, his back to me, and blew out the flame. In the ensuing darkness he paused, no doubt waiting for his eyes to adjust, as I was myself. Then he began approaching again. He would have to pass by me, no more than three feet away, to reach the door.

My hand closed on something sturdy. I moved it tentatively in case I should find it nailed down. It wasn't. I raised it carefully above my head.

There he was, so close, no more than a bulky shadow beneath a wide-brimmed hat that hid his face.

I swung the weapon down. But instead of smashing onto that hat, it hit some unseen beam overhead and was wrenched from my hand. The force of the futile swing threw me forwards. I lurched against him.

A flutter of wings and a harsh cry; a gasp, a muttered curse, a violent movement. Something struck me with terrific force in the pit of my stomach. With a cry of pain that became instead a horrible gasp, I pitched to the floor, doubled up in agony, fighting for breath that wouldn't come. Distantly I was aware of running footsteps, fading away . . .

At last my breath came more easily, the pain in my stomach subsided, and I struggled to my knees.

At that moment a hoarse laugh burst out from just above my head.

"This is the day the Lord hath made. We will rejoice and be glad in it." And in the growing light of early dawn, I saw Auld Clootie fly back into its cage.

9

I didn't sleep the rest of that night. My stomach hurt, but, more than that, my mind was in a turmoil. Again the feeling of loneliness was overpowering. I couldn't go it alone. I needed a friend.

Tod? Why not? I was sure he was the type to enjoy an adventure, and this was certainly turning out to be just that. But—could I tell him everything? Would he believe me? Only my own family believed in Father's innocence. Why should he? Well, I would just have to convince him . . .

"Someone," I said, "tried to steal the parrot last night."

"What!" Tod stopped short in the act of throwing some hay down to the animals—we were in the loft—and stared at me. "That's crazy! Why would anyone want to steal a parrot? How do you know . . . ?"

"I know," I said, "because I caught him in the act. But he knocked the wind out of me and got away."

For a moment Tod was at a loss. He looked at me in disbelief. Then he said again, "That's crazy. If you saw him, who was he? What did he look like?"

"I don't know. It was dark. I couldn't see his face. I tried to hit him with a piece of wood, but he punched me in the stomach. I couldn't get my breath for ages. And he got away."

"Is that why you looked so ill this morning, and couldn't eat any breakfast?" He was beginning to believe me. "But why didn't you wake us up, say something sooner? Or are you *used* to this sort of adventure?"

I shook my head. "It's a long story, Tod. I don't know who it was, but I would bet that he goes by the name of Smith and that he murdered Mr. Bowley."

His look of bewilderment almost made me laugh, and I felt better. "I'd best begin at the beginning. You know about the robbery at the Newboro blockhouse, and the murder of Colonel Forrester?"

"Oh yes, I know all about that, of course."

"What exactly do you know?"

"That two men broke into the blockhouse and stole a shipment of money—back-pay for the soldiers, I think. The colonel surprised them, and they killed him and got away. But one of them—an army sapper—got caught in the big storm and drowned. They found some of the money on his body, and that's how they knew he was one of the robbers. But he couldn't have done it alone. He must have had a partner who knew the money was there and where it was kept. Then one of the officers, who knew all that stuff, began to show signs of sudden wealth that he couldn't explain away. They arrested him and found him guilty. He's to hang for it. I don't know his name."

"His name," I said, "is Lieutenant James Martin. He is my father!"

"Your father!"

"Yes. And he's innocent! He never stole that money or had anything to do with it."

But Tod was sceptical. "You know what the jury said, and they heard all the evidence."

"I know. They didn't believe his story that we were given the money by someone Father had helped. The man had died and we had no way of proving the source of our new wealth."

Tod was looking at me with both curiosity and doubt.

"You really believe your pa didn't do it?"

"I *know* he didn't," I said, passionately. "He's innocent, Tod. I swear it."

"But even so—even if you're right—they're going to *hang* him!" Tod sounded ill.

I nodded reluctantly. "Unless I can find out what really happened—before the third of September."

"But how can you hope to do that?"

I shook my head. "I don't know. But because they believe my father is guilty, no one is looking for the real killer—or the money. The killer and the money are still around somewhere."

"But what can you do? Have you anything to go on?"

"Three of the men who knew about the money, including Major Hammond, live in Perth. I was on my way there when—when something happened. You see, the colonel kept a parrot in the block-house. When the thieves broke in, they not only killed the colonel, they took the parrot as well." I turned and pointed at the cage on the beam behind us. "*That* parrot. Auld Clootie."

"*That* parrot?" Tod was bewildered again. "But how do you know it's the same bird?"

"The name," I said. "D'you really think there could be two parrots with that strange name? That was the name of the colonel's parrot. Auld Clootie. I think it's Scotch for Old Devil."

"Well, I guess it's not impossible," said Tod doubtfully. "But why would they take the parrot? Sounds stupid to me."

"Because," I said, repeating my father's assumption, "it knew too much. The robbers were probably talking to each other as they went about the business of taking the money. Then suddenly the parrot spoke up, repeating everything they said. They realized it might repeat everything again when the robbery was discovered, and give them away. The only way to prevent that was to take the parrot with them."

Tod was intrigued. "That *would* give them a fright, wouldn't it? So if you're right, the sapper made off with the money. He must have—some of it, anyway. And I suppose the officer went back to his quarters so no one would suspect him. *He* couldn't keep the parrot, so the sapper must have taken it with him. Why didn't he kill it to shut it up?"

"I'm sure he meant to. But the parrot got away somehow. Perhaps when Burgess opened the cage to grab the bird, it avoided him and flew away."

"That makes sense," agreed Tod. "But now what? You've got the parrot, but so what? The robbery was weeks ago. You don't expect the bird to repeat something it heard only once, weeks ago, at this late date, do you?"

I hesitated. Put like that, my hope sounded rather futile. "That's what I'm hoping for," I admitted. "That parrot is important, I'm sure of it—for two reasons."

"What two reasons?"

"Because . . ." I hesitated again. "I don't know how to explain this, Tod, but I had this feeling, this conviction, that by coming to this area I'd find out something that would prove my father's innocence. And right away I find myself in possession of the one and only witness. That can't be a coincidence!"

"Providence," said Tod. "That's what my pa would call it." He didn't sound the least sceptical, and that encouraged me. "What's the other reason?"

"Someone else thinks the bird is important, or why did someone try to steal it last night?"

"Oh, yes, you said his name is Smith and that he murdered old Bowley. How on earth do you figure that?"

For answer I withdrew the letter from my pocket and handed it to him. "Read this," I said, "and tell me what you think."

"Where did you get this?" He started to read without waiting for an answer. "Where *did* you get it?" he repeated, wide-eyed. "In Bowley's house? Jumpin' Jehoshaphat! This man Smith *is* mighty anxious to get hold of the bird, isn't he? But do you think he would murder to get it? D'you think it was him last night?"

"I think," I said slowly, straightening things out in my own mind, "that he's the one who robbed the blockhouse and murdered the colonel. He'd be worried about what happened to the parrot when the sapper drowned and the cage was found empty. Somehow he found out that this man in Seeleys Bay had it. He tried to buy it but Hope wouldn't sell. Hope did tell him, however, what he was going to do with the bird. So he broke into Bowley's house expecting to find it there, but it hadn't arrived yet. But Bowley surprised him and there was a fight—I bet he didn't mean to kill Bowley. Then the parrot came into my possession, and your parents agreed to keep it here in the barn . . ."

"How would he know that?"

"I bet everyone in West Port knew all about that ten minutes after Walker and the doctor said I could keep him—if West Port's like any other small town."

"Oh yes, it is. You're right." Tod was looking at me with growing excitement. "You know something? If you're right, the colonel surprised this fellow and was killed. Old Bowley surprised him and was killed. *You* surprised him last night. You're lucky to be alive." His eyes were shining. "Two murders and an attempted murder. You *are* in it deep. Have you told Walker all this?"

I shook my head slowly. "No. I don't want anyone to know why the parrot is so important to me. I can't tell anyone. I'm on my own, I guess."

"No, Will. I'm with you. But it seems to me you have to get the parrot to tell you what went on the night of the robbery. How are you going to do that?"

"That's the problem," I admitted. "It only talks when it feels inclined. All I can think of to do is listen to everything the bird says and try to sift out anything that might fit."

Tod didn't look very hopeful. "Any luck yet?"

I sighed and shook my head. "Not yet. 'Up with Mackenzie,' a few Bible verses and hymns, and some gibberish about the devil's face, stuff like that. Nothing that makes much sense yet. But Tod, now that you're with me in this, there's something I want you to do for me."

"Sure. What?"

"First, don't say anything of this to anyone—not even your pa. He might not believe me." I stopped. Then I asked him bluntly. "Do you?"

He hesitated only a moment, then nodded. "*You* believe he's innocent. That's good enough for me. If I can help you prove it, I will. The letter sure asks some questions that need answers. And you're right. Pa's a good egg, but he'll want to go to the authorities and I guess we haven't time for that. What else can I do?"

"I have to meet with the constable—Walker—at two o'clock. He's coming here to question me about what happened yesterday. What I want you to do during that time is listen to everything Auld Clootie has to say. Maybe you'll notice something I've missed. Write down *everything* it says—if it talks at all. And listen for any names. That's what I'm hoping for. All right?"

"Right you are. I hope the beggar talks—for your father's sake."

10

I still wasn't getting anywhere with Auld Clootie when Mr. Munro called to say that it was a quarter to two. Dispirited, I left the bird with Tod and went into the parlour for my interview with the law.

A few minutes later there was a knock at the outer door, and Mr. Munro went to answer it. It was not Constable Walker. I was surprised to hear Major Hammond's booming voice. So he hadn't yet gone on to Perth! I wondered if his delay had anything to do with the parrot . . .

"Afternoon, Archie," the major was saying. "Anyone else here yet?"

"Anyone else?" The minister sounded puzzled.

"My wife's here of course, and the young lad Walker wants to talk to . . ."

"You mean he didn't tell you? He asked Mrs. Meadows and the doctor and me to meet him here—with you and your wife."

"Now, why in the world would he do that?" wondered Mr. Munro. "Well, come on in. No doubt we will find out in due course. Ah, here is Mrs. Meadows now. I see she's brought George and Tabitha as well."

"George too? Good. Between us we'll keep Walker on track."

They all came in then. The major nodded to me. Mrs. Meadows smiled at me and turned to the man with her. He was tall and heavy with iron grey hair, a stubborn chin, and piercing eyes. "George, this is Will Martin, the boy I was telling you about."

"How d'you do, Will?" His grip was firm. "Bad experience for you, finding a dead body. Funny how it happened. Well, no doubt we'll hear all the details when Walker arrives."

Tabitha was there too, and she smiled at me—a momentary smile—but to me it lit up the room. She didn't say anything, simply sat down primly between her mother and her stepfather and looked demure and ladylike. But I thought of that mischievous twinkle I had caught when we first met. I wondered if her parents were aware of its existence.

Mrs. Munro came in from the kitchen and looked around in surprise at the assembled guests.

"Well, isn't this an unexpected treat," she

beamed. "I must put the kettle on. You will all stay for tea after Mr. Walker has finished his business, won't you?"

"I would love to," said Mrs. Meadows. "But I'm afraid Tabby and George won't be able to wait. Tabby is going to stay with her aunt in Buttermilk Falls for a few days. She will have to go home to change. They will be riding down."

"Buttermilk Falls? What a pretty name. You know, I've heard of it before but I have no idea where it is."

"It's on Devil Lake," said George Meadows. "The north end. It's off the main channel but the lake boats go in there through Loon Lake. In fact, the *Bytown* was built there."

"But didn't Mrs. Meadows say that you were riding rather than going by steamer?"

Tabitha was about to speak but her stepfather overrode her.

"We missed the boat," he said, "because I wanted to find out why Walker wanted to speak to my wife. Anyway, it's a much shorter trip by land to Devil Lake. The boat goes the long way round and takes forever, but by land it's no more than nine or ten miles. And there's a decent trail through the bush. Not safe for a young girl alone, of course, so I'm going with her and coming straight back."

Walker came in without knocking, followed by the doctor.

"Thank you all for coming," said the constable. "Hello, George. Nice to see you."

"I don't see why you called this gathering," grumbled Mr. Meadows. "How can my wife be of any help? You're investigating the murder of old Bowley, aren't you?"

"That's right. I'll explain in a minute. I wonder if I could sit at the table, Mrs. Munro. Thank you." Walker drew a notebook from his pocket, while Doctor Farr found a seat in the corner and began to fill a long-stemmed pipe with tobacco. He looked at me and nodded.

"Hello, lad. Did the parrot behave itself last night? Disturb the neighbours?"

"No," I said, "it was very good—"

"Now," interrupted Constable Walker, clearing his throat with authority, "as you are aware, Mr. Bowley was murdered. First I want to know what each of you knows about the old chap."

"That's absurd," objected the major impatiently. "You probably know him better than any of us."

"That's as may be," said Walker testily. "Come on. Anyone. Mr. Munro? You visited him regularly. There are those rumours that he had money. Was there any truth in them?"

The minister shook his head. "I doubt it very much. He never struck me as being miserly. If he had money, I think he would have spent it on his house and on better food. I don't think anyone really believed those tales."

"Ha!" said Walker, as if he had scored a point. "Anyone disagree with that? No, I thought not. The only motive I can think of is robbery, but no one in town would try to rob Bowley. Therefore, the murderer must have been a stranger, one who may have heard the rumours and believed them."

"This is all speculation," grumbled Major Hammond. "What I want to know is why you want to talk to *us*. The lad found the body, and called the minister and the doctor. Fine. But where do Mrs. Meadows and I come into it?"

"I'm coming to that, Major. Doctor Farr, when was Bowley murdered?"

"I can't say exactly, of course," said the doctor placidly. "But I can assure you it was sometime between midnight and four a.m."

"Aha! Now." Walker turned an accusing eye on me. "Where were *you* at that time, Mr. Martin?"

I was startled. I thought he had given up on me as a suspect long ago.

"On board the *Bytown*," I said. "As these people can testify."

"But can they? Mrs. Meadows, tell me what you know about this young man."

"Oh, he was on the *Bytown*, all right. We were on the dock at Newboro waiting to board when Will joined us. He wanted to ask the major something."

"How about you, Major? And Mr. Munro? Is that the way it was?"

"Certainly," said the major.

"Absolutely," agreed the minister.

"Right!" said Walker. "But where did he come from? We have only his word that he arrived on the steamer. He could easily have been in West Port, murdered Bowley, and then walked to Newboro in plenty of time to join you on the jetty."

I stared at him, mouth agape, almost too fascinated by his theory to feel alarmed. "You—you must be joking," I managed.

"I'm not joking. Why did you leave the boat after saying you were going to stay on board and go to Perth? He did, did he not, Major? And why did you go to Bowley's house?"

"I left the boat," I said, trying to still a rising panic, "because I thought West Port was a pretty place and I wanted to see more of it. And I went to Bowley's house to deliver a parrot that had been left on the wharf. It was addressed to him, but he hadn't come to collect it."

"That's the flimsiest reason I've ever heard of. Why would *you*—"

"Just a minute." The calm voice of the minister broke in. "All the lad has to do is prove he came in on the steamer. If he did, he could not possibly have been the murderer. Can you do that, Will?"

"I—yes, I must be able to. People saw me. The captain. And the purser. They could tell you . . ."

"They're all miles away by now."

"Then there's my ticket," I remembered, relieved. "It has the date on it. The date I purchased it in Jones Falls. I'll fetch it . . ."

"You won't have to." We all turned and looked in surprise at Tabitha. She was speaking for the first time. "Will came in on the steamer. I know. I was on the dock when she came in and I saw him on the deck. He came in on the *Bytown*."

There was a moment of silence. Walker began to sputter in frustration.

"Look, miss, you can't be sure."

"Are you calling her a liar?" Mr. Meadows's jaw jutted threateningly. "If she says she saw him on the boat, that's all there is to it. Will Martin didn't murder Bowley. Couldn't have. You'll have to look somewhere else. Is that all you wanted us for?" '

"Yes. No. Just a minute. I have to get this down in writing for my superiors." He took up his pen and turned to me, his face expressionless. "Now, your full name, please."

I was absorbed in trying to catch Tabitha's eye, to thank her for her help, and answered absently.

"John William Martin."

"Place and date of birth?"

"Brockville. May twenty-third, 1831."

"Name and occupation of father?"

"Father?" I stared at my inquisitor. Now it would all come out. Now they would all know. Should I lie? No, I wouldn't. I took a deep breath, and spoke defiantly.

"Lieutenant James Martin, Royal Engineers."

11

There was a moment of utter silence, of suspended breath. The atmosphere was suddenly charged with tension.

"Lieutenant James Martin!" Major Hammond was staring at me with undisguised hostility. His voice was soft but full of venom. Before he could say anything more, another voice repeated the name, with contempt. It was Mr. Meadows.

"Lieutenant Martin. The murderer!"

The blood drained from my face. I sprang up, toppling my chair, my fists clenched. But Constable Walker grabbed my arm.

"The murderer! You said yesterday that you were not related to him," he challenged.

"No, I didn't," I retorted, controlling my voice with an effort. "You asked me if I was related to the killer of Colonel Forrester. I'm not. My father had nothing to do with the robbery or the killing."

"The jury said different." The doctor was eyeing me appraisingly through a haze of smoke.

"The jury was wrong," I said shortly.

"Juries seldom make mistakes," snapped George Meadows. "They base their verdict on facts. Martin! Of course! I knew you looked familiar. You look like your father."

I was surprised. "You knew him?"

"Oh yes, I knew him. I worked with him on several of the locks, especially the Isthmus."

"Then you didn't know him very well, or you would know he couldn't kill anyone."

Before Mr. Meadows could reply, the quiet voice of the minister interrupted. "Will," he said, "your father is due to be—is due to die in a very short time. Why are you here?"

I hesitated, then looked around at them all boldly. "To prove his innocence," I said. "The real murderer is still around somewhere. I intend to find him."

"Then you're wasting your time," growled the major. "Better go home and be with your father. Better accept the fact that he's guilty."

But the doctor spoke mildly. "Maybe you'll think I'm crazy, but I'm inclined to go along with the boy. I knew your father too, lad. I doubt if he ever killed anyone—except in the line of duty, of course. He *was* a soldier.

I turned to him gratefully. "Not even then. He was never in combat. But how did you know him?"

"I knew all the officers at the Isthmus. I was on call whenever military doctors were unavailable. Yes, I knew the colonel, and I knew his parrot too. Did you know he owned a parrot?"

"A parrot?" I mustn't let on that I knew the identity of the bird. "Did he own a parrot?"

"Yes, he did. As we all know, eh, Major? George? And the odd thing is that the parrot's name was Auld Clootie."

"Auld Clootie!" It struck me that I was sounding like a parrot myself, repeating everything I heard. "You mean, that parrot I delivered to Mr. Bowley—"

"—was the colonel's bird," broke in the major. "That's right. He was an easy bird to teach. The colonel taught him to say 'Up with Mackenzie' just to shock his Tory friends. And I for one resent the fact that the colonel's parrot is in the hands of the son of his murderer. You have no right to the bird."

"My fault entirely," said the doctor hastily. "Ben and I didn't know what to do with the creature, and the boy offered to take it. Of course we didn't know Will's identity then. I suppose it belongs to any relatives old Bowley might have, if we ever trace any."

"Enough of this," snapped Walker. "Who cares what happens to a stupid bird? I'll confiscate it myself. Where is the parrot now?"

"Out in our barn," said the minister.

"Right. Would you be so kind as to fetch it for me?"

"Certainly."

I watched in dismay as the minister left on his errand. I had only one hope left, a very slim one. Maybe Tod had learned something from the bird in my absence . . .

"Maybe the parrot can give you some clues, Ben," said the doctor with a chuckle. "He talks, you know. Has he much of a vocabulary, Will?"

"No, he doesn't say much. The words are clear but they don't make any sense. He seems to say a lot about the devil and he repeats some hymns and Bible verses."

"I shouldn't think he learned *those* in the army, eh, Major? Must have been his last owner who taught him some religion."

"I would be interested in knowing who *that* was too," said Walker. "Why was he sending the parrot to old Bowley?"

"I don't suppose we'll ever know that, Ben. But we do know the parrot didn't kill the old chap. And neither did Will here, evidently. And that's all you have to worry about."

"Maybe so, but you never know what an investigation will turn up." The constable shut his notebook and stood up. "My superiors will have to worry about the case from now on. They will probably want to talk to you all sooner or later."

"Oh, Mr. Walker, couldn't you stay for a cup of tea?" urged Mrs. Munro. "And some cakes?"

"Thank you, no. I'll just see how Mr. Munro is coming with that parrot."

"We will be going home too," said George Meadows. "Come along, Tabitha."

They stood up as well and made for the door. I wanted to have a quick word with Tabitha to thank her for her help—if she would still listen to me after learning my identity. I rose quickly. "I'll give Mr. Munro a hand with the parrot," I said.

"Please come back for some tea," pleaded Mrs. Munro. I was grateful. She, at least, didn't hold my father's conviction against me.

"I will, thanks."

I followed George Meadows and Tabitha to the door. Mr. Meadows turned then to have a word with Walker. For just a moment I was alone with the girl.

"Tabitha," I said, "I want to thank you for coming to my aid."

She looked at me amusedly with those green eyes. "You *were* on the steamer, weren't you?"

I stared at her. "You mean, you didn't really see me?"

There was a touch of laughter in her voice. "I lied," she said. "But I knew you couldn't have done it." Then she was gone.

12

"I'm sorry, Will." Tod spread his hands helplessly and shook his head. "Nothing."

My heart sank even further. "Nothing *at all*? You mean, Auld Clootie didn't say anything?"

I had found Tod sitting in the hayloft where I had left him. The spot on the beam where the birdcage had sat was conspicuously empty.

"Oh, it spoke now and then. 'Auld Clootie knows,' that sort of stuff. But it didn't mention any names—except for Mackenzie, of course. 'Up with Mackenzie.' You know all about that." He dragged a crumpled piece of paper from his pocket and handed it to me. "That's it."

There wasn't much on it. "That's everything?"

"Except for its favourite hymn and rebel slogan. I didn't bother writing them down."

I glanced at the short list.

"'Wait till you see the devil's face.' We've heard that one before—too often. What's this? 'By the light of the moon'?"

Tod nodded. "It tried to sing that one. At least, I guess you'd call it singing. That's the first line of the song, you know."

Tod launched into a vigorous imitation of the parrot singing and I broke in hastily. "Yes, of course. And what's this? 'Come on, stupid bird, say something worthwhile.' Auld Clootie said *that*?"

Tod grinned. "Oh yes, it did. Guess where Auld Clootie heard *that*?"

I sighed. I crumpled up the paper and threw it away. "Thanks anyway, Tod. I guess I've been wrong all along."

Tod was silent for a moment, then said hesitantly, "I guess you were expecting too much from that bird."

He was right, of course. I *was* expecting too much from a parrot, rationally speaking. But I never should have started out on this quest at all, rationally speaking, with nothing to go on but a hunch. Tod was right, but I didn't want to admit it.

"There has to be something special about that bird, or why did someone kill Bowley for it? Or, if I'm wrong about that, at least we know someone tried to steal it from your barn."

"Well," said Tod, "I've been thinking about that, and I have an idea. It may be crazy. Want to hear it?"

"Sure. Anything."

"'Come on, stupid bird, say something worthwhile.' I said that, Will, and Auld Clootie repeated it then and there. But my guess is that the bird'll never say it again—unless someone says it first. We can't expect a parrot to repeat something a month later. I'll bet Auld Clootie's forgotten what I said already." He hesitated, looking at me anxiously. "See what I mean?"

I nodded heavily. "It only overheard the robbers once, a long time ago, so we can't expect it to repeat anything they said at this late date. I know that. Those things the bird does say, it was taught to say, probably by repetition. The colonel taught it to say 'Up with Mackenzie'—Major Hammond said so. And we know Nathaniel Hope taught it the hymns and Bible verses. And he probably heard 'by the light of the moon' a hundred times . . ."

"So," Tod said eagerly, "someone must have taught Auld Clootie to say those things about the devil. Right?"

"Yes, I guess so. But who? And why? What does it mean?"

"Well, this is my idea. The robber took the parrot along to act as a messenger."

"Huh?"

"Look. Mr. Smith—we've agreed he's the other thief, haven't we? He wants to find the parrot, not because it will give him away, but because it's the only one who can tell him where the money is. I know," he said, seeing my disbelief, "it's strange, but listen. Let's suppose the robbers have got the money out of the safe or wherever it was stored and are about to get away when the colonel walks in! There's a struggle. They kill him. They probably didn't mean to, but he's dead anyway. Now all hell's going to break loose. It's one thing to steal, but it's something else to murder a colonel! The country's going to be crawling with army and police. They likely meant to hide the money nearby at first, but with all this excitement no place close is going to be safe. They panic. I bet they even think of leaving the loot and just getting out of there. But then they calm down a bit. They've come this far; they might as well go all the way. The officer—it's likely one of the lieutenants. Who did you say they were?"

"Merriton and Blake."

"We'll say it's Blake. My guess is the sapper is on leave or has been let go and won't be missed for a few days. So Blake tells him to take the loot and get away, fast, while he goes back to his quarters so he'll have an alibi. The sapper was a local chap, if I remember right, so he'll have no trouble hiding out. He's to take what money he needs to get over the border, and to hide the rest—bury it, probably— where Blake can find it later. Somewhere miles away. There's a problem, of course."

I grunted. "There's a problem, all right. How is Blake to know where to find the loot?"

He grinned. "That's where the parrot comes in. It was right there all the time. Maybe it spoke up about then. Anyway, it gave Blake an idea. I take it all the staff were familiar with the bird—how easy it is to teach it words?"

I nodded. "I think so."

"So before the sapper leaves the country he's to take a day or two and repeat over and over again a clue that will tell Blake where to look. Then he's to leave the parrot where Blake can find it later. My guess would be one of those huts the army is abandoning all over the place."

"But why not just leave the loot there—or a note saying where it is?"

He looked at me pityingly. "Because all those places will be searched, of course. But what will they do when all they find is a parrot? They'll return it to the blockhouse, of course. And only Blake will be able to make any sense out of what Auld Clootie says. There. What do you think?"

I was fascinated. "I think it would take a genius to think up something like that."

"That's right," grinned Tod. "And Blake and I are both geniuses."

"And of course," I said, taking up the story, "it didn't work out because sometime between hiding the money and leaving the parrot they were caught in the storm, the sapper drowned, and the parrot flew away."

"Right. And Blake is at his wits' end because there's a fortune out there somewhere and only a bird knows where it is. So he has to find it, even if he has to kill to get it."

I nodded slowly. It was fantastic, but it fit. it could explain everything.

"As a matter of fact," I mused, "no one seems to have paid any attention to the fact that the parrot was missing. Well, let's suppose you're right. What do we know?"

Tod sighed. "Not much," he admitted. "We can account for everything Auld Clootie says except about the devil."

"Yes, the devil. That keeps popping up, doesn't it? 'Wait till you see the devil's face.' If you're right, that must be a clue. The devil's face. What the devil does it mean? The officer has to look for a devil's face. Where are you likely to see *that* around here?"

Tod looked blank. "Hanged if *I* know."

"For a clue, it doesn't help much, does it? It must mean more to the man it was intended for than it does to us. That is, if we're on the right track, of course. Devil . . . Now why does that sound familiar?"

"Familiar?" Tod laughed. "From the parrot, of course. Besides, that's its name, isn't it, 'Old Devil'?"

"No, no," I said impatiently. "Something else. Oh, yes, I remember. Something Mr. Meadows said. He said Tabitha was going to stay with her aunt at Buttermilk Falls. And Buttermilk Falls is on Devil Lake. Devil Lake! D'you hear that? And he said that to get there, the boats have to go through Loon Lake. And Loon Lake is where the sapper's body was found." I was beginning to get excited. "Tod, maybe we're onto something here. Have you ever heard of Devil Lake?"

"Oh yes, I think so. But there are a lot of lakes around here."

"Right, and I bet they're all named after people or animals or birds. Why do you suppose this one was named after Old Nick? Could it be because there's a devil's face somewhere around it? A rock formation, for instance?"

Tod was excited. "It could be. Sure, why not? And that could be where the money is hidden. What about it, Will? D'you think we've really hit on it?"

I was pacing again, hope and doubt in a bitter battle. Was I grasping at straws? Was I letting my imagination run away with my common sense? I stopped and took a deep breath.

"Tod," I said. "Time's running out. I have to be home on the second of September—*early* on the second. There's no time to go to Perth. It's too far, too hard to reach by boat. The only thing left is a devil's face. It's that or nothing. How about it? Will you come with me?"

Tod grinned. "Just try to stop me."

It wasn't easy, but we persuaded Tod's parents to let him go on a fishing expedition with me to Devil Lake. Once convinced, however, Mr. Munro entered into the spirit of the thing as if he were going along. They already had a tent. He bought Tod a new fising rod and made sure that we had everything else we might need, and promised to wake us so we could make an early start.

At an early breakfast the next morning, Mr. Munro had news for us.

"The parrot's gone," he said. "It disappeared from Walker's shed some time last night."

My eyes met Tod's. "Mr. Smith has got him," I whispered, "and that means he's got the secret."

Tod nodded. His face was white, but his eyes gleamed with excitement.

"Now it's a race," he said. "Who'll be the first to find the devil's face?"

13

We could have walked to Devil Lake in less than three hours, but because of the tent, the sleeping bags, and the fishing gear, walking was out of the question. We had to go by canal steamer.

We reached Newboro by noon, but the steamer was headed down the canal to Kingston and no boat was scheduled to take the side trip in through Loon Lake. Eventually, we found a canoe for hire and paddled in to our destination. But by the time we arrived, we had lost a whole day.

When we pulled the canoe out of the water at Buttermilk Falls, writhing grey and black clouds had turned the sky into a battlefield. Everything was deathly still, except for the water slapping nervously against the dock. We could sense, however, that the wind was not far away, waiting for the perfect moment to unleash an attack.

"I think we'd better find shelter for the night." I caught the attention of a dock worker. "Is there a hotel here?"

He shook his head. "No, but there's a boarding house up on the hill. The last house, white clapboard. Mrs. Grange. Better than a hotel. But you'd best hurry. We're in for a storm."

We shouldered our gear and hurried up the steep hill. On any other occasion I would have stopped to admire the falls tumbling in white froth over the precipice, but there was no time . . .

We reached the last house, dumped our gear thankfully on the verandah, and knocked at the door.

The next moment I was standing face to face with Tabitha Meadows!

"For goodness' sake!" I stammered.

She seemed just as surprised as I was. "Will!" she said. "And Tod! What are you two doing here?"

For a moment I was too taken aback to answer, so Tod spoke up for us. "We're going fishing on Devil Lake, but a storm's coming up and we want a room for the night. We were told that this is Mrs. Grange's boarding house."

"Yes, it is. Mrs. Grange is my aunt—my step-aunt, actually." But Tabitha spoke absently. She was staring at me in disbelief and with something like revulsion. "Your father is going to be hanged and you're going *fishing*?"

"No! No, I'm not—"

"Tabby, who is it, dear?" A motherly figure, flour-dusted, appeared behind her.

"Two boys—from West Port. Tod Munro and Will—Will Martin. This is my aunt, Mrs. Grange. They want a room for the night, and then they're going *fishing*!" She turned away, her back eloquent with disapproval. She was disappointed in me. I knew it.

I wanted to call after her, but Mrs. Grange was speaking. "Come on in, boys. Your gear should be safe here on the porch. We have plenty of room— only one boarder at present. You're just in time, too. We're going to have a storm any minute."

Even as she spoke, lightning flared across the western sky and some distant thunder rumbled. The topmost leaves on a big elm nearby rustled nervously.

"Tabitha? Now, where did she go?"

"Yes, Auntie?" She came back, not looking at me.

"Show the boys up to the big room, will you, dear? Then come down and help me with the tea."

"Yes. This way." Without another word, she led us up a wide staircase and opened the door into a large room with two beds, each covered in a patchwork quilt. A rag rug lay on the floor. But I hardly noticed what the room looked like. I just wanted to square myself with her.

"Tabitha," I said urgently, "we're not really going fishing. That's just a front. I'm still trying to clear my father."

"Here? In Buttermilk Falls?" She sounded incredulous. "How are you going to do that here?"

"It's a long story. But I want to tell you. You helped me once. Maybe you can help me again."

"Me?" She sounded doubtful. "I don't see what you're doing here. And besides, I have to go help Auntie with the tea. I'll call you when it's ready. She'll expect you to join us."

"But look," I said, "it's—oh, I can't explain in a few minutes. Promise me you'll listen when we have time?"

She looked at me curiously, then finally nodded. "All right." She turned to go.

"Just one thing," I said hurriedly. "Have you ever heard of a devil's face? Probably somewhere on Devil Lake?"

"A *what*?" She was bewildered. "Did you say a devil's face?"

"Sounds crazy, doesn't it, but we're serious. It's a clue. We'll explain later. It doesn't mean anything to you, eh?"

She shook her head. "No, nothing like that. It might mean something to Aunt Emmie. She's lived here all her life. Or to our boarder, Mr. Warp. He knows everything there is to know about Devil Lake."

"Good. We'll ask him." Or maybe we won't, I suddenly thought. I didn't want everyone to know what we were looking for. At that moment I happened to glance out the window, but where I expected to see the water of Devil Lake, I saw only logs—lots of them, stretching from shore to shore.

"Is that Devil Lake?"

"Part of it. The mill pond. Those logs are waiting to go through the mill. You can't see the main part of the lake from here. It's beyond that point. I have to go. Come on down when you hear the bell."

She left then, and thunder rumbled louder as the storm drew closer. The light in the room faded.

A table covered with snowy linen was set for five in the dining room. Tod and I were waiting to be seated when the wind suddenly arrived.

It attacked with a rush, hurling a cataract of rain against the house. The big elm in the front yard writhed and the window panes rattled. Jagged lightning split the gloom, followed at once by a crash of thunder.

The door opened and a man came in—a cadaverous wraith of a man. My immediate impression was of points—a pointed beard, a sharp nose, black hair that came to a point in the middle of his forehead, and pointed ears like misplaced horns. He floated across the room as if his skeletal body was too negligible to be affected by gravity. He was passing in front of the window when lightning flared again. I swear I saw the flash right through the man's body.

"Tod and Will, will you sit here?" Mrs. Grange set a huge teapot on the table. "And you here, Mr. Warp. Have you been introduced? This is our boarder, Mr. Warp. Tod and Will from West Port." She seated the man opposite me and I found myself looking into his eyes. They reflected a sudden flash of lightning.

"Good," he said in a sepulchral voice. "It's good to have company. Are you staying long?"

"No," I said, "just overnight. We're going camping tomorrow. And fishing. On Devil Lake."

A crash of thunder lingered and reverberated. The room darkened.

"Dear me," said Mrs. Grange. "It *is* gloomy. Tabby dear, bring the lamp."

There were scones dripping in butter, and oatcakes and tarts and homemade bread, but I'm afraid they were wasted on me. I was scarcely aware of what I ate, or of the storm raging outside, or even of Tabitha seated beside me. I was only conscious of that strange man opposite. He seemed to be looking at me all the time, the flickering lamplight mirrored in his eyes.

"So you're going fishing on Devil Lake, are you?" he said eventually. "Why?"

"Why?" His abrupt question startled me. "To catch fish, of course."

"Of course," he agreed. "But if that's all, why Devil Lake? Why not Loon Lake, or Mud Lake? Or, if you're from West Port, the Rideau?"

"Oh," I said, vaguely "just for a change. And out of curiosity. Can you tell me, sir, where Devil Lake got its name?"

A blast of wind shook the house. The big elm tossed and twisted, raking its branches across the verandah roof.

"Now, why would you want to know that?"

Before I could answer, Mrs. Grange spoke up. I had almost forgotten she—or anyone else—was in the room. "I think the Indians had a name for it. They believed it was haunted by evil spirits, and 'devil' is someone's translation of the Indian name. Is that not right, Mr. Warp?"

He looked at her for a long moment. He didn't answer her question directly. "Evil spirits," he repeated in a hollow voice. "Oh yes, *they* decide who's going out on Devil Lake. We could see *this* storm coming, but sometimes storms come up like that." He snapped his fingers. "And they catch people like you and me out on the lake, and maybe we don't make it to shore. But not the Indians. They can smell a storm coming. They don't go out on the lake in the full moon either."

I couldn't drag my eyes away from that pinched face, those sunken eyes. "They don't? Why not?"

"The full moon does things to you when there is evil around. And there is evil on Devil Lake, believe me. Camp if you like, fish if you want to. But whatever you do, when the moon is full, as it soon will be, don't—" His words were lost in a crash of thunder. The house trembled under a wild lashing of rain that drummed on the roof like a stampede of buffalo. The lamp flame wavered wildly in a sudden draught.

We all held our breath. Eventually, the flame revived, rekindling some life in Mr. Warp's dead eyes.

"We're going camping," I said recklessly. "And we'll be looking for the devil's face." I wanted to see his reaction.

There was a moment's silence, and then a low moan filled the room, a moan that swelled into a crash of thunder that rolled and echoed into the highest heaven. At the same instant there was a flash of lightning, a tinkle of shattered glass, and the door exploded inward with a thud. A gust of wind swept through the room, extinguishing the lamp.

I was vaguely aware that Mrs. Grange and Tabitha had jumped up to close the door. But I couldn't move. My wrist was clamped fast in a cold, viselike grip. Mr. Warp, leaning across the table, had me in his grasp.

"Take my advice, young man. Forget about the devil's face."

I stared at him, hypnotized. "Then there *is* a devil's face?"

"Of course there is." His grip was like steel on my wrist. "And people see it sometimes, and when they do—they die!"

"That—that's crazy." I could only manage a whisper.

"Is it? Three people—no, four people have seen the devil's face. One fell between the logs and was crushed. The cook at one of the lumber shanties saw it as well—and was killed by a bear. And I—I have seen the devil's face."

"But you aren't dead." Or was he? For a moment

the wild thought crossed my mind that I was talking to a corpse.

"No," he said. "I'm not dead. But I'm dying. I'll not last much longer."

I could believe that. "But you've seen it. Tell me where it is."

"No!" His voice was suddenly sharp, decisive. "I will not send another to his death."

I was trying to collect my scattered wits when Tod spoke, and his voice sounded quite normal. "But that's still only three. You said there were four people."

"That's right. There was another, several weeks ago. A soldier . . ."

"I remember that." Mrs. Grange was talking quite calmly, like Tod, as if nothing strange was going on. Was it all my imagination? "You mean the man with the parrot?"

"Yes. The man with the parrot. He saw the devil's face on Devil Lake. He told me so. The next day he drowned in Loon Lake."

The man with the parrot! The sapper—it had to be! I felt my face flush with excitement. "And the parrot?" I felt as if I were someone else, looking at myself from a great distance. "What about the parrot? Do you suppose it saw the face too?"

My question must have sounded queer to the others. But if it sounded strange to Mr. Warp, he didn't say so.

"It must have. That's why it disappeared. That's

why it hasn't been seen since. I told you—if you see the face, you die."

And suddenly the spell was broken. Mr. Warp's hypnotizing face and voice no longer held me capture. His grip on my wrist was easily broken. And outside, an ordinary, if severe, storm was gradually diminishing.

Because *I* knew the parrot had not died.

14

"Now," said Tabitha, "can you tell me what's going on?"

Tod and I were sitting in our room, still somewhat bemused by Mr. Warp's words, when Tabitha knocked and came in.

"I'll try," I said. "It's rather complicated." She listened as I struggled to put into words the driving force that had started me on my quest, and the belief that a parrot held the key to success.

"A parrot!" she exclaimed at last. "Are you really counting on the word of a parrot?"

I hesitated only a moment. "Yes, I am. A parrot's word is all I've got. It's that or nothing, because time is running out. There *is* a devil's face. Mr.

Warp said so. Remember the soldier he mentioned—the one with the parrot? That has to be the man who stole the money from the blockhouse. He was *here* between the time the money was stolen and the time he drowned. And Mr. Warp said the man had seen the devil's face. To me that suggests the sapper hid the wooden box here—perhaps somewhere near the devil's face. Then he taught the parrot what to say to his accomplice. Anyway, Auld Clootie's words are the only clue we have to go on, so Tod and I are going to look for a devil's face."

"Even if it kills us," said Tod, only half in jest. Don't forget what Mr. Warp said, Will: 'People die when they see the devil's face.'"

Tabitha was serious. "I asked Aunt Emmie about that."

"What did she say?"

"It's true, those people he mentioned *did* die. But so did lots of other people who, as far as we know, never saw any such thing. Lumbering is dangerous work and there's no doctor here—though Doctor Farr comes down from West Port at least once a week. And it's true the Indians don't go out on the lake in the moonlight because they fear evil spirits. The lumbermen don't go out either, though it's not because of superstition, they say, but because they work hard all day, and night is for sleeping. Besides, they figure, why take a chance? Just in case the Indians are right."

"Well," I said, "we're not worried about evil spirits. I don't see much point in looking for something in the dark, anyway. If we can't find the devil's face in the daylight, we might as well forget it."

"You said maybe I could help," Tabitha reminded me. "What can I do?"

"Whoever stole the parrot is going to be down here looking for the money too," I predicted. "Can you keep a lookout for us? Let us know if someone comes to Buttermilk Falls with a parrot?"

"But we can't count on that," Tod pointed out. "Whoever it is might have figured out the message a lot faster than we did. Then he won't need the parrot anymore. He'll leave it behind, or"—he mimicked Auld Clootie's harsh voice—"wring his filthy neck!"

"Never mind," said Tabitha. "I'll watch for strangers, and check to see who goes out on the lake. Not many people are fishing at this time of year, and the lumbermen are all busy in the mill or on the scows." She hesitated. "I've been on the lake before—when Uncle Amos was alive. He used to take me fishing. I would be glad to come with you if I could help."

I looked at her standing there, in her pale yellow dress that showed off the rich tones of her hair and brightened the green eyes that looked challengingly into mine. She was a different girl from the one who had sat meekly between her mother and her stepfather in the Munros' parlour. Once again she reminded me of Sarah. I would have loved her to come, but of course her aunt would never allow it.

"We'll be camping overnight," I reminded her.

"It wouldn't be proper. But do you remember seeing anything like a devil's face when you were out with your uncle?"

"No," she said. "But it's a big lake, with islands and bays. It could take you a long time. If I can help, I'll be here. And if I do see someone—someone suspicious—how will I get the message to you?"

"We'll have to find a way to reach you, I guess. We'll come back here soon. And—do you think your aunt could supply us with some food—enough for two days? I have plenty of money." Ironically, that same money that had sealed Father's fate.

"Oh, yes, I'm sure she could. Is that all?"

"Yes, I think so. Thanks—" I hesitated—"Tabby."

She smiled, and was gone.

15

When we set out early in the morning to find a devil's face, we didn't expect it to be an easy task. "*Look* for the devil's face," the parrot had advised. Whatever the devil's face was, we guessed it wouldn't be in plain view or easily recognizable. We had to look for it. No, I expected a difficult task—but had I known how difficult, I would have been tempted to give up in despair.

As Tabitha had warned us, we had to get past the millpond before we reached the main lake itself. Nonetheless, as we paddled past a point of land, we were dismayed to see the rest of the lake open up miles to the west.

"Holy cow!" groaned Tod. "Look at that! It's an *ocean!*"

Tabitha had told us that Devil Lake had many islands and bays, but "many" was an understatement, to say the least. Dozens of islands dotted the water, and there was no knowing how many bays and inlets and peninsulas each one harboured, all adding many miles of shoreline to be searched. In how much time? Two days at the most.

For a moment I stared at the lake with a sinking heart. I should have been entranced by the beauty around me—the shimmering blue of the water, the luxurious greens of the foliage on the shorelines and hills—but I could hardly take the loveliness in. Instead I saw miles and miles to be searched, and heard in my head the ominous sound of a clock, ticking off the seconds to September the third.

"What now, Will? Should we set up camp first?"

Tod's words brought me back to the task at hand. I nodded heavily. "I guess so. How about on that island ahead? Looks like a clearing at the top of the hill. Might be a good lookout."

All day we paddled the lake—or rather, a small part of it. We explored bays that stretched deep into the countryside, long, narrow peninsulas, and a veritable archipelago of islands. By the end of the day we felt as if we had barely started. Part of our problem, of course, was that we weren't sure what we were looking for. Scarred cliffs and rock formations, of which there were plenty, seemed to hold the most promise. One cliff in particular, not far along the north shore, attracted us. I *wanted* to see a face on that seamed and riven crag, but finally had to admit that the most eager effort of my imagination could not produce one.

Tod pointed out a hillside where the lumbermen had left a patchwork of trees and stumps. To our anxious eyes, as the afternoon waned, it looked a little like a face with one eye. But who knew when exactly the trees had been cut? Surely, we agreed, we were looking for something in the landscape that was more permanent.

The water had turned blood red, reflecting the setting sun behind us, when we headed back to camp. We paddled silently, too disheartened to speak. Another precious day had gone by and I was no closer to saving my father's life. One more day was all I could afford, and then I had to go home to be with Sarah. For all we knew, the elusive devil's face could still be miles away, at the far end of the lake.

It was a quiet night. Clouds piled in from the west, leaving us in a black world, relieved only by the leaping light from our fire. Sitting there in the brooding silence, we heard the haunting call of the loon, and then the eerie howl of wolves starting on the near shore. As the cry was caught up by other packs far away, the night shivered with their unearthly chorus. Then the brilliant moon, slightly lopsided, sailed clear, extinguishing all the stars except at the farthest horizon, and casting shadows that moved and whispered in the motionless air.

Tod stirred, yawning. "I'm going to turn in. Tomorrow, Will. Tomorrow, we'll find it. I can feel it in my bones. We're going to have a bit of luck at last."

"Of course we are," I said, but they were empty words.

I have no idea how long I sat by the fire. I do know I was tortured by thoughts of home—of Father in his cell, and Sarah—what was Sarah doing? Was she wondering about me? Had she given up hope of my return in time? *Would* I return in time? *Yes!* Whatever happened, I had to reach home to be with my family before time ran out.

The last embers were fading reluctantly when I heard it.

I sat bolt upright, my mouth open in mid-yawn. I stared into the shadowed splendour of the night, searching here, peering there. I leaped to my feet, ready to plunge down the hill and launch the canoe and go in search of what I had heard. Then common sense stopped me. How could I guess from what direction, or what distance, the sound had come? But one thing I knew for certain: Auld Clootie was somewhere on Devil Lake. There was no mistaking that heart-stopping screech.

As I stood there, eyes straining into the night, I saw something—a shadow? an apparition?—glide across the carpet of moonlight and melt into the dark shadows cast by the far shore. No, not an apparition. A canoe. A canoe with two people in it, on the lake in the moonlight, defying Mr. Warp's evil spirits.

I knew then. I knew, with rising elation, that I was on the right track. The parrot was here and the devil's face must be here somewhere. All I had to do was find it, to prove my father's innocence. And to do that I had to beat these other people to it, for I had no doubt they were looking for the same thing. With Tod's help, I could do it. But not tonight. I quelled an impulse to rouse Tod then and there and set off in pursuit. It would have to wait until daylight could show us the way.

I slept little that night, and was up before the sun. "He's here, Tod. Auld Clootie." I was shaking him awake. "I heard him last night. And there was a canoe out on the lake. It's a real race now. We have to get going."

"Any idea who was in the canoe?" Tod was struggling into his pants. "So I guess I was wrong. He didn't wring the parrot's neck after all. Maybe we should have checked with Tabitha last night. She'll know who it is."

"Knowing who won't be any help anyway. Whoever it is, we've got to find the devil's face first. They started out last night, but they can't have found anything yet, I figure, because they'll need daylight to search. In fact, we may have the advantage because we're pretty certain it's not at this end of the lake."

"Did you say 'they'?"

"Yes." I frowned. "That's true, there were *two* figures in the canoe last night."

"Mr. Smith and an accomplice," suggested Tod.

"Must be. I wonder who? Well, it doesn't really matter right now."

"So what are we going to do? What if we meet them out there?"

Tod was dressed now. I snatched up our food basket and we started down the hill to where our canoe was beached. "Mr. Smith must know who you are. If he sees you he'll know darn well what you're here for. And don't forget that Mr. Smith killed the colonel and Mr. Bowley, and knocked you out when you surprised him in the barn."

"I'm not likely to forget that." I was mulling the problem over as we pushed off from shore. "We've got to keep a sharp lookout, and if we see them, we'll have to keep well away so they don't recognize us. You can troll, Tod, while I paddle. After all, we're just fishing. I'm going to take us down past where we left off yesterday. With any luck we'll pass them while they're in one of the bays. All right? We're off."

We started out buoyed by my belief that that we had an advantage over our adversaries, and by Tod's hunch that today we would be successful. We headed south, away from the direction in which I had seen the canoe the previous night, around a string of islands already checked, then headed in a westerly direction. Soon we were in new territory where, once again, there were deep bays and rocky points to explore. Here and there low walls of weathered stone lined the lake. Their cracks and scars were reflected in the mirror-calm surface to form wonderful, symmetrical patterns.

Once, in these designs, I saw a face, with a lowered brow, a long nose, and a grim mouth. I stared at it in momentary excitement, but when I pointed it out to Tod I was already beginning to have my doubts. He shook his head. "Too small," he said.

"Why?" I didn't want to be disappointed. "No one said it had to be big."

"Well, all right, but I don't see how anything could be hidden there. Just what are we looking for anyway?"

"I thought you knew that," I said irritably. "The money, of course. Or something to tell us where it is."

We swung in close. When the wash of the canoe disturbed the surface, the face vanished. The mouth had only been a reflection of the heavy brow.

Oddly enough, I wasn't too down-hearted. Not then. Rather, I was encouraged. There would be more and better faces in the rocks ahead. Or so I told myself.

But there weren't. We saw nothing resembling a face. My spirits drooped. It was maybe an hour later when Tod spotted the house.

At first only the roof was visible above some scrub trees, then we saw that it was a log cabin, set in a valley between low, wooded hills.

"A trapper's cabin," guessed Tod, not particularly interested.

"I bet you're right!" I was excited. "Come on, Tod. We've got to investigate."

"Why?" Tod was surprised. "We're looking for a face, not a cabin."

"But if it's a trapper, he'll know the lake. He'll know if there's anything like a face anywhere on the lake."

"Hey, that's right. Maybe it's an Indian. They know better about these things."

So we found a place to beach the canoe and approached the cabin while a friendly grey jay watched us with inquisitive black eyes.

A string of traps hanging by the door and some beaver pelts stretched out on a form confirmed that this was a trapper's home. We approached with rising hopes, but there was no one in sight. No one answered our calls. I pushed open the door, remembering with a shudder opening that other door and finding a bloody corpse. I was both relieved and disappointed to find the place empty.

I wished we could stay there and await his return, but there was no way of knowing how long that would be.

"We can come back this way if we haven't found anything," Tod said, noticing my dejection. "He'll likely be back by then."

Encouraged by this, we went on to the end of the lake and explored a bay that went deep into the countryside, with no results. We even paddled up to the river that fed the lake until our way was barred by a falls. When we turned back, the sun was already behind the trees on the western hill.

I realized then that we had seen no sign of that other canoe. I wasn't sure if that was good or not. They would be looking where we had looked yesterday, in the many bays closest to civilization, so we could easily miss them. Or—this was the disquieting thought—had they found something we had missed? I couldn't see how that was possible, but it made sweat start on my brow that had nothing to do with my paddling efforts.

"Come on, Tod," I urged, though I knew very well that he was doing his utmost, "we've got to go back and hope that trapper's back by now."

He wasn't. There was no sign of life at his cabin. I called, and went inside, and into the nearby trees, lingering, reluctant to leave, because I knew he was my last hope. But at last Tod took my arm without a word and led me back to the canoe, for light was fading fast.

We had not seen the other canoe. Neither had we found anything that looked like a face, devil's or not.

I knew, with the bitter taste of defeat, that I had failed.

16

My last day of grace was gone, and I had nothing to show for it. Tomorrow morning I had to take the first boat out of Buttermilk Falls to travel home, where I would have to admit to Sarah that I had been wrong. My hunch must have been nothing more than my cowardly refusal to face Father's death. I had only one thing to be thankful for. Neither Sarah nor my father had expected me to succeed. They wouldn't be disappointed.

We were approaching our island for the last time. We had already decided to break camp immediately and return to Buttermilk Falls for the night. That way, I would be ready for the first boat whenever it sailed.

"Will," said Tod suddenly, "there's someone at our camp!"

I looked up sharply. The island was just ahead. In the fading light I could see our clearing near the top of the hill, and the shape of our tent.

"I don't see anyone," I said, straining my eyes against the shadows.

"I can't see him now, but he's there all right."

Someone at our camp! I felt a growing excitement, a sudden nervousness in my gut. I could think of only one person who might be interested in our movements. Mr. Smith! And surely he would only be interested if he had failed to find the money. Did he think that we had beaten him to it? Was he now searching our camp for the wooden box?

Tod had stopped paddling. "What are we going to do?" His voice was tense.

"Go up and find out what he wants," I said, trying to sound matter-of-fact despite the quiver in my voice.

"But suppose it's Mr. Smith. He could kill us, Will."

"There are two of us, Tod," I pointed out, my words sounding braver than I felt. "We'll be ready for him. I hope it *is* Mr. Smith. He's my last hope."

"There could be two of them too, Will. Remember, you saw *two* men in the canoe last night."

I had forgotten that. "You're right . . . let's keep paddling, Tod. We don't want him to know we've seen him."

"We could just keep on going to town," suggested

Tod. "Forget the tent. I can come back for it anytime."

"No," I said decisively. "I can't do that. As long as there is hope of proving my father innocent, I have to keep searching for the money. If I have to take chances, I will. You can drop me off at the island and keep going if you want to."

"I'll do no such thing," he snapped. "I can be as big a fool as you can." He plunged his paddle into the water, anger masking a growing fear. "I just hope you have a plan. I don't."

"Thanks, Tod," I said gratefully, and tried to decide what we should do. "He won't know our usual landing spot," I reasoned aloud, "so he won't be suspicious if we go around to the far side. There's more cover there. Have you got your jack knife?"

"Yes, it's here. How about you?"

"No. I guess I left mine at the tent. I'll have to find a good piece of wood for a club. That shouldn't be difficult. There's plenty of wood around."

"You can have my knife. I'd hate to stick it into anyone. If I had a choice, I'd rather hit 'em over the head."

"All right, but keep it till we land. Have you seen him again?"

"No, but he's there, all right. I definitely saw someone. And his friend may be there too."

I altered course to take us around the head of the island, and we pulled in close to the shoreline. For a moment our tent was in plain sight, in spite of the gathering gloom. There was no sign of life. Then, as we paddled on, the camp was hidden again behind the trees. I hoped Tod had not been mistaken. I desperately wanted to meet Mr. Smith.

We found a spot where the shore shelved down into the water, and pulled the canoe out. Were we being watched? We had no way of knowing. Perhaps our uninvited guest had followed our progress around the island and was even now watching us from the shelter of the trees. But no, I told myself, he was much more likely to hide near our campsite so that he—or they?—could surprise us when we stepped out into the open . . .

"All right, Tod. I'll go straight up this way. You go over the hill and up the far side. I'll give you a couple of minutes."

"What's the plan?"

"If he doesn't know we've seen him," I said, "he'll be expecting us to walk up quite openly. Which is what I'll do. But you should be as quiet as you can and keep to cover. Find yourself a thick branch and then climb the hill, keeping hidden till we see what happens. If I need you, come over fast."

He nodded and handed me his knife. I took it reluctantly. The idea of stabbing someone sickened me, but even so, holding the weapon gave me a measure of reassurance. Tod left, then, and I took a few moments to move the canoe to a different position, whistling loudly in a clumsy attempt to explain to any listening ears why we were delaying our approach. Then I started up the hill, knife concealed in my hand. Dried leaves rustled loudly around my feet, twigs snapped like pistol shots, and I started to whistle again, hoping my noisy advance would drown out any sound Tod might be making on the other side of the hill.

The light ahead brightened as the trees thinned, and I could see the tent. I hesitated, my knees feeling suddenly weak, as I searched for some sign of the intruder. Had Tod been wrong? Well, there was only one way to find out.

I stepped into the clearing. I was only steps away from the traces of our fire, but the short distance seemed to take ages to cross. I felt a prickly sensation down my spine. Was there a club, or a knife, or even a pistol waiting to welcome me?

Then a voice behind me said quietly, "Hello, Will. I thought you'd never get here."

17

I jumped a foot and swung around, dropping my knife.

"Tabitha!"

She was standing in the door of the tent, dressed in riding habit and sweater, and towelling her hair as if her presence was the most natural thing in the world.

"Tabitha!" I said again. "How did you get here?"

"I rode Ajax along the shore as far as I could and then swam across. It isn't far. I brought a change of clothing in a waterproof. Will, I've got news for you. I don't think it can wait. Where's Tod?"

"He's coming. Tod!" I shouted. "Come on out. It's Tabitha." Then I explained. "We saw someone here and didn't know who it could be. We never thought of *you*. We didn't want to take any chances, so Tod's creeping up the hill with a club, and I was going to protect myself with that." I pointed to the knife at my feet. "You gave us a scare."

"I'm sorry. I didn't mean to."

Tod came out from the trees. "Gee, Tabitha, I'm glad to see you. What's going on, anyway?"

"She's brought some news," I said. "I think I can guess part of it. The parrot's here, right? I heard it screeching last night. Can you tell us who brought it?"

"Yes. Two people." She hesitated for a long moment, obviously troubled. "Will, I couldn't believe it. It was Major Hammond—and my step-father."

"What!"

The major and Mr. Meadows! Could this possibly mean that *they* were behind this whole mess? Could one of them be 'Mr. Smith'?

"D'you hear that?" Tod had grabbed my arm. "*They've* got the parrot. Why? That doesn't make sense."

I shook my head. "Maybe it does." Major Hammond was one of the original suspects, even though he had an alibi—and Mr. Meadows was that alibi! Had they been in this together right from the start? Either one of them could have killed Mr. Bowley and still have been on the dock when the canal boat came in. Walker had demonstrated that when he had tried to implicate me.

"D'you think it could have been one of them who tried to steal the parrot?" wondered Tod.

I remembered that shadowy figure in the dark barn, bent over under the low ceiling, and I nodded. "Either one."

And then it hit me!

Someone else—it didn't matter who—was guilty. My father was innocent! I had been right all along. I had done everything right. But—my soaring spirits came down with a crash. I hadn't proved anything. And time had run out.

Tod turned to Tabitha. "Where did they get the parrot?"

"Major Hammond found it flying loose."

"That's not what we heard," I muttered. "It was stolen from Walker's shed," I gulped. "You—you know what this means, Tabitha?"

She nodded miserably. "Yes. It looks as if they're the ones who robbed the blockhouse. And killed Mr. Bowley." She shook her head. "I can't believe that. I don't get along very well with my stepfather, and he's beastly to my mother sometimes, but I can't believe he would *kill* anyone."

I couldn't blame her for feeling that way, but the evidence looked grim. "What happened?" I asked.

"They arrived yesterday by boat—with the parrot. They're staying at Aunt Emmie's for a few days. I told my aunt I was going to stay with my friend Mary for the night, and came down here as fast as I could. So they have no idea I'm here."

"Do they know *we're* here?"

She shook her head. "I don't think so. You were never mentioned."

"Are they there now—at your aunt's?"

"They weren't when I left. They were out somewhere last night. They must have come in late—after I was in bed. Then they went out again this morning early, and still hadn't come back when I left. They didn't take the parrot with them this time."

I nodded. It all fit. They were out looking for the devil's face. But what good was that news to me? No one was going to believe me if I tried to accuse them. I had no proof. Unless I caught Major Hammond and Mr. Meadows with the stolen money, I might as well forget it.

"Will." Tabitha broke in on my despairing thoughts. "There's something else. I listened to the parrot today. I may have got something."

"Oh?" I wasn't too hopeful. "What did it say?"

"Well, I think you know about Mackenzie and the Bible verses, and Auld Clootie's nose—"

I laughed briefly. "Not his nose, Tabitha. He's not talking about his beak. What he's saying is, 'Auld Clootie knows.'"

"Sometimes. But not always. Sometimes it's saying 'Auld Clootie's nose.' I'm certain of it."

"Well, I suppose it could be. But I don't see how that can help us now. It might mean something if we ever find the devil's face. But we haven't found it yet, and we've run out of time."

"Wait a minute. There's more. 'Wait till you see the devil's face'—"

"We know that."

"But it also says 'by the light of the moon.'"

"We know that too." Tod pointed out. "It's the first line of a song. I expect Auld Clootie's heard it dozens of times." I was disappointed, even though I hadn't really expected anything new.

But Tabitha caught my arm. Her green eyes were bright with excitement, even in the gloom.

"Don't you see? The parrot put the two together: 'Wait till you see the devil's face by the light of the moon.'"

"Oh!" I digested that information thoughtfully, then shook my head. "How can you see anything in the moonlight that you can't see in broad daylight? It doesn't make sense."

"Oh yes, it does," she said eagerly. "Haven't you ever been out in the moonlight? *Bright* moonlight? It casts shadows. Things look quite different by moonlight."

Things look different by moonlight . . . Yes, she was quite right, now that I thought about it.

". . . a cliffside," she was saying. "You know— the granite cliffs with clefts and bumps? There are some of those around the lake. I've seen them."

"Yes, there are." I felt a tinge of excitement. "One in particular. You know the one I mean, Tod?"

"Sure. The big one on the north shore. It's worth a try, Will. Tonight. The moon is full. It will be as bright as day before long."

I glanced up to where the moon waited. Right now it looked like little more than a piece of tissue paper that the first puff of wind could blow away. But in an hour or so, it would sweep on stage in its full glory. "We'll do it, Tod. We'll go out and take a look. It can't do any harm."

"Harm?" Tod sounded uncomfortable. "What was it the old man—Warp—said about being out on the lake in the full moon?"

"Forget *that*. That was nonsense. Tabby, what are you going to do? You can stay here . . ."

"I'm coming with you, of course." It was a flat statement of fact, leaving no room for argument. I didn't try.

"Okay. In about an hour . . ."

18

The moon was as round and bright as a newly minted silver dollar as we launched our canoe onto the shimmering lake. I scarcely noticed it. I ignored too something dark and menacing that blotted out the stars in the west. I paid no attention to a sudden gust of wind that soughed through the pines, shivered across the lake, and evaporated as abruptly as it had materialized. I was barely aware of a distant, ominous rumbling.

There was no room for any of these things in my mind. Instead there was elation over the proof of my father's innocence, excitement over the possibility that we might soon discover the incriminating money, and a terrible awareness of the shortage of time. And over it all, the obscene shape of the gallows.

We passed the mouth of a small bay, then a larger one. A cliff loomed ahead, a black shadow, facing the lake. To get a proper look at it in the moonlight, we would have to swing out. I altered course.

Something changed. A dark shadow crept across the water. I looked up. A raven-black cloud was reaching for the moon. A sudden gust of wind whipped across the lake, plucking at my shirt, wetting my face. There was a distant murmur like the sound of booming surf, then a jagged streak of lightning tore the western sky apart.

"Will," said Tod anxiously, "I think we'd better go back and wait this out. We're in for a storm."

I hesitated. The night wasn't completely dark yet. There was still a faint glow of moonlight through the distended cloud. I had to see its effect on the cliff ahead. This was my only chance.

"Will!" said Tabitha urgently. "We can come back . . ."

I knew we should go back—but not yet. Just one more minute. The moon hadn't surrendered yet. It was struggling against clutching clouds, trying to break free. The light on the water faded, brightened, faded again. Then, for just a moment, the moon sailed clear, splashing its radiance across the lake. I turned to look at the cliff.

For a moment, and a moment only, the deep clefts and ridged projections on the cliff were in stark relief. And in that moment I saw it. A face was leering at me—a face with deep-sunk eyes, a long nose, a pair of horns.

"Look!" I cried hoarsely. "There on the cliff! The devil's face!"

Then the clouds rolled over the moon, and the vision was gone.

There was a moment of utter stillness. Then lightning slashed across the sky, thunder crashed over us, and a screaming torrent broke loose. The wind shrieked out of the west, tearing at us, driving a wall of rain into our faces.

"Paddle!" I yelled, plunging mine into the water to bring us around. For a moment we were beam-on to the rising waves, heeling far over. "Hang on!" Then we were around, pointed back to camp.

The wind-whipped waves should have followed us then, sweeping us back the way we had come. Instead they rolled over our stern, soaking us, and then came at us from the beam, lifting us, almost overturning us. Rain and waves ran over us like water over Buttermilk Falls. Every few minutes dazzling jags of lightning lit the terrifying scene in a blaze of stark white light, then plunged us into total blackness so that we could see nothing at all. The canoe seemed to be alive, doing its own version of a frenzied dance.

"Can't you *steer* the blasted thing?" There was terror in Tod's yell.

Breathless, I shook my head helplessly and tried once again to counter-balance against the powerful thrust of the waves. Tabitha shouted something, but the storm snatched away her words. Abruptly, the wind spun the canoe around and, to our horror, we found ourselves headed out into the wild, angry lake. Then the forces changed their mind, toying with us, almost swamping us, spinning us around so that the cliff now towered above us.

"Backpaddle!" I screamed.

Tod and Tabitha must have felt helpless, flung about by the storm, depending on my steering experience to bring them to safety. It is as well they didn't know how limited that experience was.

Then, in a moment of sudden calm, when the wind and the waves seemed to be catching their breath, our paddles bit deep and we pulled ourselves away from danger. Quickly, I steered the canoe along the shoreline, and for a moment we rushed along the base of the cliff. If we could only keep going for another minute . . .

The cliff vanished, and before us appeared a bay, a haven.

"Paddle on the right side," I yelled. The canoe obediently turned inland, just as the wind, with renewed effort, screamed down on us. The bay was wide, and offered only limited shelter, but it was enough for us to control the canoe.

Cliffs soared above us here too. We plunged along as if we were riding a bucking steed, looking for a place to land. Then the shoreline disappeared, and we found ourselves entering a narrow gap into a secluded little bay. Although the rain still fell on us, the storm's fury was wasted on the surrounding hills.

We were too exhausted to speak. Without a word we pulled for the nearest shore. Again sheer cliffs ringed the water so we had to run along the base until at last our keel bumped on an unseen shelf of rock. We stumbled out into knee-deep water and pulled the canoe up onto the shore.

We huddled together, trying to shelter each other from the rain and wind.

"Did you see it?" I asked. My voice was little more than a croak.

"Yes," said Tabitha. "I saw it. And for a while I thought Mr. Warp was right, and that the devil's face was going to claim three more victims."

"That wouldn't be fair," said Tod. "*I* didn't see any face. So if there are going to be any more victims, I better not be one of them. Maybe I'm the one who saved you two." He grinned. "Where was the face, anyway?"

"On the cliffside. The moonlight and shadows . . ." My voice died away. A strange, ghostly ringing sound came, and faded, and came again. It began on the high breath of the wind, shivering eerily, then died away, a hollow dirge.

"What's *that*?" I wondered.

But before anyone could reply, the world was split wide open. A blaze of white light leaped from the black heavens and stabbed at a tall pine high on the cliff above us. A ball of fire split the tree from the topmost twig to the base of the trunk. In an instant, in spite of the rain, the pine became a blazing torch. We watched in terror as, for a moment, it writhed in flames. Then it slowly began to tilt—right above us.

If I could have made a sound, I would have screamed. Fortunately, Tabitha still had a voice, and her yell jolted us out of petrified terror. "Run!" she cried. She grabbed my arm, then lost it as I stumbled over a rock or stick. I rolled, scrambled to my feet, fell again, and watched the fiery horror fall out of the sky towards me.

At the last moment I rolled again. I felt the heat from the burning tree as it crashed, the tips of its branches inches from my face. For a minute the flames leaped into the air, and then abruptly disappeared. Smoke rose from the black and twisted remains.

I tried to call out, but no sound came from my parched throat. I tried to move, trembling violently, but there was no strength in my arms. I took a deep, ragged breath.

"Will? Tod?" Thank heaven! Tabitha at least had survived. Before I could answer, Tod's voice came from somewhere beyond the skeleton of the tree.

"Here, Tabitha. Where's Will?"

I gasped with relief, my voice returned, and strength came back into my body. "I'm here. Anyone hurt?"

"You don't need to worry about me," said Tod. "*I* didn't see any face, remember? Where are you, Tabitha?"

We came together, then, at the end of the blackened tree, and huddled together. The storm was beginning to weaken. Lightning still flashed, but the thunder was taking longer and longer to reach us. The rain had dissolved into a heavy mist. A faint light shone through thinning clouds.

We listened as a final gust of wind rushed through the trees. Then, once again, we heard that hollow, ringing dirge, like a death knell.

Tabitha shivered. "What do we do now?" she asked through chattering teeth.

"The storm's about over," I said with forced cheerfulness. "I suggest we go back to the camp to dry off and change our clothes. I've got some extra gear if you've used yours all up, Tabitha. Then we can come back and try to figure out the secret of the devil's face."

Tod had left us for a moment and was walking the length of the fallen tree, looking for something. "I don't think we're going back to camp for a long time, Will. Not by water, anyway."

"Why? What do you mean?"

"I mean the canoe—or what's left of it—is somewhere under this tree."

19

"Oh no!" Tabitha and I rushed over to where we'd pulled the canoe ashore, and stared in horror. Under the blackened branches, we could see only the smashed keel and the charred remains of one of the paddles.

"*Now* what?" I asked.

No one had an answer.

So near, and yet so far! We had found the devil's face, leering over the lake, and we had no way of reaching it. Oh, we weren't marooned. We were on the mainland, and could walk back to Buttermilk Falls—a long walk through bush, over hills, across streams . . . And then we could borrow another canoe and come back. But all that would take time, and time had nearly run out. The shadow of the gallows loomed over everything.

Into my tortured thoughts came that dismal sound again. I don't know when it started. I just know it was suddenly there, insinuating itself into my hearing, a hollow ringing, like the sound of doom.

"What *is* that noise?"

"A bell," suggested Tod doubtfully. "That's what it sounds like to me. But why would someone be ringing a bell—"

"Of course!" broke in Tabitha. "You're right, Tod. It's a dinner bell."

"Oh sure," scoffed Tod. "A dinner bell in the middle of the bush in the middle of the night?"

"No, I mean it. I don't think anyone is ringing that bell—I think it's just swinging in the wind. There are lumbermen's shanties around here somewhere, where they eat and sleep when they're working in the forest. And there's a big bell the cook rings when the meals are ready." Her voice grew more excited. "And where there are shanties, there are bunks and blankets and stoves . . ."

"Just what we need!" cried Tod. "What direction is that noise coming from, anyway?" None of us could be sure, but it was obvious that we would have to climb up to the top of the cliff that circled the bay. The sheer rockface above us was out of the question, but farther along we might well find gentler slopes that we could scale. I looked anxiously skywards. "The moon's going to come out again soon," Tod predicted. "Let's see if we can follow that sound."

Moments later, the moon pushed the clouds back and shone down on a dripping world. As we made our way along the shore, a light wind shook the rain from the trees, drenching us anew, but it also, every now and then, rang the bell tantalizingly. We soon found a slope that we could climb easily enough into woodland, and paused to listen. We decided the sound was coming from the west, and set out, squelching. In a few minutes we emerged into a moon-splashed open space, with a long, solid shadow lurking behind it. The bell rang again, clearly.

"That's it," said Tod in anticipation. "The bunkhouse. Let's hope we can get inside."

That proved easier than we dared hope. The door was unlocked. We pushed into darkness that was partly relieved by moonlight reaching in through numerous windows. Long tables and benches told us that we were in the mess hall.

"There must be lamps here somewhere."

"Here they are," announced Tod. "*And* a box of lucifers."

Off the mess hall we discovered two rooms. One was the kitchen, where Tod and I set about lighting a fire in the big stove. The other was where the men slept in rows of double bunks. Tabitha went in there first, and emerged wrapped in a blanket, carrying her clothes. She hung them over the stove and coaxed the fire along while Tod and I followed her example.

We were crossing the floor, carrying our clothes while trying to hold blankets about ourselves, when my foot hit something, sending it skittering across the floor and under the table. I retrieved it. It was a flat, rusty tin box. I left it on the table while we arranged our clothes around the warming stove.

I picked the box up again, idly curious, a few minutes later when the three of us sat around the table. What a strange-looking trio we were! We had tried to dry ourselves with flour sacks, but still looked as if we had just stepped from our baths. Tabitha's dark hair was a wild mop.

"What's in the box?" she asked.

For answer I opened it. There was a paper inside. I unfolded it carefully and spread it out in front of us. A moment passed before I realized just what it was. Then I caught my breath.

"What is it?" asked Tod, leaning over for a better look. "Just two or three lines. What are those words?"

"It looks like a map of sorts," guessed Tabitha. "*Is* it a map, Will?"

I nodded wordlessly.

There was a horizontal line labelled "cliff top." On one side of it were several more lines, but these were wavy. Across them was printed, in an unschooled hand, the word "face," with an arrow pointing to the horizontal line. On the other side of it was a series of tiny arrows ending in an X. Beside them were the words "twenty paces." That was all.

"Those wavy lines," said Tod, beginning to get excited, "those must be the lake, and the word 'face' must mean the devil's face—the one you two saw on the cliff. You've found the map, Will! We don't need to go out on the water again after all. The stolen money's here, on the cliff top. All we have to do is find the face from above. That should be easy. It can't be far from here. Now, what does 'twenty pases' mean? Oh, *paces*, of course. Twenty paces from the edge of the cliff, and there it is!"

I nodded slowly, my own excitement subsiding. "There it *was*, Tod." I sighed. "We're too late."

"What do you mean? Why do you say that?"

I held up the tin box. "How do you suppose this got here? The thief didn't leave it here weeks ago. Someone else must have found it recently and left it here by mistake. And anyone who found this map and knew what it was all about would have no trouble following it and finding the money. Perhaps this box was found in a cleft where the nose on the face is. Remember 'Auld Clootie's nose'? I guess they figured out the parrot's message a lot quicker than we did."

"But when?" asked Tod. "When did they come here and get it?"

I shrugged. "Today, I guess. They were out last night, remember?—and must have found the face in the moonlight. Then they must have come here today while we were down at the other end of the lake. They had lots of time." I turned to Tabitha. "You said Major Hammond and—and Mr. Meadows were still out when you left?"

She nodded reluctantly. "They were supposed to

stay overnight at the boarding house, so Aunt Emmie was expecting them back."

"Did they come by boat or on horseback?"

"By boat. Doctor Farr always comes on horseback. He's there now. It's his day to look after his Buttermilk Falls patients, but the major and my stepfather came by boat. And there won't be a boat out until tomorrow afternoon."

"The *afternoon*? Are you sure? I was counting on getting away early in the morning. I have to be back in Brockville tomorrow."

She shook her head. "Tomorrow is Thursday. There's no boat until the afternoon."

"We're not going to be back early anyway," Tod pointed out. "We have a long walk in the morning—we'd never find our way in the dark. But we should be back in Buttermilk Falls before Major Hammond and Mr. Meadows leave—time to find out if they really do have the money."

I had to let it go at that. Everything was happening at the same time. If they *did* have the money, would I have time to do anything about it? My father was to hang Friday morning. That left only tomorrow to get back to Buttermilk Falls and to catch the culprits with the stolen money. Then what? Who would listen to me? How could I convince anyone in authority of my father's innocence in time to save his life? Or get back to Brockville in time to be with Sarah?

I waited impatiently for the dawn.

20

We were up before dawn. A quick search revealed nothing to eat, no tea or coffee to make, but thankfully our clothes were dry, at least. Though the sun hadn't yet appeared when we stepped out into the cool morning, it was spreading a rosy light into the eastern sky.

"Don't you think we should follow that map," said Tod, "just in case the money *hasn't* been dug up? When we're so close we might as well."

I hesitated. I didn't want to waste any more time. But he was right. We would be foolish not to make sure.

We set out in the direction of the lake, climbing upwards through the trees. We emerged high above the lake with a sheer drop below us. This should be it, I thought. The face should be on this particular cliff that dropped away to the water. Before us a point of rock jutted out, a point almost severed from the mainland by a wide, deep cleft.

There are lots of such clefts all over this rock-bound country, and lots of boulders on the shores where great chunks have broken away over the years. I knew that, but I didn't give it a second thought. I just wanted to look over the edge and make sure we were standing above the devil's face—on his head, so to speak.

The cliff looked different from here, of course, but a glance over the lake assured me that this was the one on which Tabitha and I had seen the face the night before, and must be the one on the map.

Satisfied, I turned. Again, I noticed how wide and deep this cleft was, and I thought, fleetingly, that it would soon split wide open and part of the cliff would break off and fall into the lake below. I had no idea *how* soon.

Something suddenly gave beneath my feet and I looked down, curious. I had thought I was standing on solid rock, not something that would shift under my weight. I *was* on solid rock. But it was moving.

Too late, I knew with sudden terror that the sharp point of rock was breaking away from the cliff. In panic, I leaped for safety. But the rock was going, and I was going with it.

My clutching fingers grabbed for anything they

could hold onto. I heard Tabitha scream. And from below came the crash of rock hitting rock.

I caught something. One hand clutched some kind of plant. It threatened to come loose, then held—for a moment, at least. My other hand clawed desperately at the edge of the cliff. My face was mashed against the cold rock face, and my feet dangled terrifyingly. Nothing but an empty void stretched between me and the cruel rocks somewhere below.

"Hang on!" cried Tod, from somewhere above. I had every intention of heeding his advice for as long as possible, but for how long could I? I could feel the plant giving, ever so slightly. The fingertips on my other hand couldn't hold on much longer. I tried desperately to discover a foothold, but my scrabbling feet found nothing. Every movement shot pain through my fingers. I couldn't hold on much longer.

The plant gave way. Just at that moment, a hand grabbed mine. Another clamped onto my wrist. And I was hanging there, held only by Tod and Tabitha.

"Can you pull me up?" My voice was muffled against the cold, wet rock and I didn't know if they could hear me.

There was a moment's pause. I could feel their grip loosening. This is it, I thought. The end . . .

"There's no way." Tod was breathless. "We're leaning as far over the cliff as we can. There's no leverage. Nothing to anchor . . . We need a rope . . ."

But we don't *have* a rope! I wanted to scream at them. I choked down the words. They were doing everything they could. It wasn't their fault.

Suddenly I was calm. So this was the end. Below the rocks were waiting for me—waiting to kill me, or to maim me for life. But that wasn't the worst of it. I had failed my father and Sarah. I had come to the end of my quest, and just when victory seemed within my grasp, it was snatched from me. I could see my father mounting the steps to the gallows, never knowing what had happened to his only son. I could see Sarah standing alone, all alone.

"Will!" Tod was shouting again, his voice harsh with the strain. "We're going to have to let you go." They had done their best. "There are rocks below. But you can miss them."

I could *miss* them? A sudden hope . . .

"Listen," he was saying. "You've got to kick yourself *away*, as far out from the cliff as you can. D'you hear me? Can you do that?"

"Yes! Yes, I can." I bent my knees to bring my feet up, thrusting them against the rock. I must have put more strain on my friends, but they held on.

"Good. Now kick. Hard. You should clear the rocks, and the water looks plenty deep. When I say *go*. Are you ready?"

"Yes," I gasped. This was the moment.

"All right. One. Two. Three. *Go*."

At the moment they released my wrists, I kicked as hard as I could, launching myself out into space, turning a complete somersault in the air, plunging down, down, down . . .

I hit water. Hard. But it was water, not rock. I was plunging down into the cool water of Devil Lake. In my terror I had forgotten to take a deep breath, and now my lungs were ready to explode. But the knowledge I was alive gave me strength. Desperately I kicked against my downward motion, and at last began pushing up again. I burst out into precious air, and gulped deep, cool draughts of it.

It was several seconds, I guess, before I heard it: the sound of cheering from far above. There were Tod and Tabitha, leaning out over the edge of the cliff, waving and calling to me.

I waved back, eternally grateful to them for saving my life. And then I looked at the cliff. It had changed. The fall of the rock had altered the devil's face. In the bright morning light it was plain and unmistakable, even though the horns had disappeared with the fall of rock. It would no longer need the shadows cast by the moon to reveal itself.

I had to swim some distance before I found a bank low enough to negotiate. I crawled out, a band of pain across my shoulders where I had hit the water. Tabitha was there waiting for me. She reached out a hand to help me.

"Thank God you're all right, Will."

"Thank *you*," I said. "If you and Tod hadn't held onto me I'd have fallen into the rocks. Where's Tod?"

"Looking for the money—or where the map says it is. Or was. Do you want to go up and look? It means climbing up to the top of the cliff again."

I shook my head. We had a long walk ahead of us, and I was pretty sure the money was long gone. I sat on a boulder, working my shoulders in an effort to relieve the pain. "We'll wait. It shouldn't take him long."

In a few minutes we heard him coming noisily down the hill. The look on his face told us he had been disappointed.

He gripped my hand. "Will! You gave us a scare. Are you sure you're all right?"

"I gave *you* a scare!" I laughed rather shakily. "Yes, I'm fine—thanks to you and Tabitha. You saved my life. The money's gone—right?"

He nodded. "I found the place, exactly where the map said it would be. Someone beat us to it. There was a pretty big hole. You can still see the shape of the box. They didn't bother to fill it in. It's gone, all right."

"Fine." At least we knew. "Then it must be somewhere in Buttermilk Falls and we'll have to find it. Let's go."

21

This was strange country to all of us and, though it would have been shorter to cut across the hills and through the woods, we didn't dare take a chance on getting lost. So we had to follow the shore line, stumbling over roots, thrusting our way through tangled undergrowth, now high above the lake, then on the very shores where otters plunged into the water, started by our sudden appearance. We had to go around a small lake caused by a beaver dam, and then through a swamp we could have avoided if there had been time, sinking to our calves in murky water.

Blue jays scolded us, squirrels chattered, and white-tailed deer fled gracefully before us when we came to an open space. We paid no attention.

We arrived at last, breathless, at the pond on the opposite shore from the village. Logs waiting to be fed into the mill almost covered the surface. We went around this, keeping to the trees, and came out within earshot of the falls. Here we paused to take stock of our situation.

The village was very quiet, with not a soul in sight. We could hear the saws whining in the mill.

"What will the major think if he sees us?" wondered Tod. I knew he didn't mention Mr. Meadows for Tabitha's sake.

"I don't know." I was just trying to puzzle that out myself. Would he guess that we were looking for the devil's face? Would it matter if he did?

"They've found the money," said Tabitha quietly. "They won't care what we do now. But I think we should stay out of sight as long as we can. I know how to get to Auntie's house without being seen. Follow me."

She led us through a fringe of trees behind the houses until we came to the last one—Mrs. Grange's boarding house.

We stopped then. I wasn't sure what to do now. We knew who the thieves were but we had no evidence. Who would believe me rather than Major Hammond? But I had to so *something*.

"I think we should go in and see if we can find out anything—if the major's still there or if he's gone."

Tabitha nodded. "I won't go in with you. I don't

want Aunt Emmie or my stepfather to see me. I'd have too much explaining to do. Ajax—my horse— is still where I left him on the shore opposite your camp. I think I'd better go and get him."

"Won't that take a long time?"

"No. There's a path all the way and we'll come back like the wind. But Will, what are you going to *do*?"

"Why don't we tell your aunt we're hungry?" suggested Tod. "It's true enough. I bet she'll ask us in for some grub and that'll give us a chance to check up on the major and—" he stopped, embarrassed. "On the major," he repeated.

"That's a great idea." I wanted to get going. "We'll do that. What we do afterwards depends on what we find out—whether they're guilty or not." I had no doubt about that but I could see that Tabitha did. "If they have stolen the money."

"Well," she said unhappily, "if they dug up a box of money, it will still be in the house. Their rooms are at the top of the stairs."

"I'll look there if I have a chance. Tabby, we'll be here when you come back."

For a moment her hand squeezed mine. "Good luck," she whispered, and was gone.

Tod and I reconnoitred Mrs. Grange's house from the shelter of the trees for a few moments. The only sign of life was a horse hitched to the verandah post, saddlebags bulging, tail twitching lazily. Doctor Farr's horse, I remembered. There was no sign of our suspects.

We went to the door and knocked.

"Well, boys, it's you again," said Mrs. Grange with a smile. "Looking very hungry, I must say. Come on in. We will soon remedy that. How's the fishing?"

"Not too good," admitted Tod. "We're not very good fishermen, Mrs. Grange. We would love some home cooking for a change. Is Tabitha here?"

"No, she went to stay with a friend overnight." She sighed. "It's too bad. Her stepfather—my brother—is here, and they don't get along very well. She's a high-spirited girl and he tries to smother her. His name is George Meadows. If you're from West Port, I expect you know him."

"Yes, we know him. Is he in just now?"

"No. He and his friend Major Hammond have gone up to the mill. I don't expect them back for an hour or so. They're leaving this afternoon. Doctor Farr might drop in. Do you know him too? It looks as if the devil's face is claiming another victim, if you can credit such things."

"Pardon?" We were bewildered. "What do you mean?"

"Mr. Warp. Remember him? Our strange little boarder. You met him here at supper the other night. His time is up, I'm afraid. The doctor is attending him, but there's nothing more he can do."

Tod and I exchanged glances. So another person who had seen the face was about to pay the price— if, as Mrs. Grange said, you can credit such things. And Tabitha and I had seen it too. I couldn't help feeling just a little uncomfortable—for a moment, at least.

It wasn't lunchtime, and breakfast was long past, but Mrs. Grange insisted on making some pancakes, while I fretted and tried to hide my impatience. I needed an excuse to go upstairs and search the visitors' rooms but I couldn't think of one. I went out once, supposedly to go to the privy, but really to see if there was any way I could possibly climb up to one of the upper windows. There wasn't.

It didn't take Mrs. Grange long to prepare the food, but it seemed like forever. I'm sure it was delicious. Tod at least enjoyed those pancakes swimming in maple syrup, and the bread and jam. When Mrs. Grange's back was turned he made a quick sandwich and shoved it in his pocket with a wink at me. "For Tabby," he whispered.

It was an immense relief when she said, "Well, boys, I'm going up to the store to do some shopping. You are welcome to make yourselves at home, if you want to stay around for a while."

"Thank you," I said, and, if she was surprised at the fervent way I said it, she didn't let on. "We'll likely see you again before we go home."

"I expect you will." Her eyes twinkled. "I never knew growing boys to be satisfied with camp food for long. There's always bread and jam here for you, if nothing else."

"Now, Tod," I said, when she had gone, "I think you'd better go back to Tabitha with that sandwich.

She should be back by now. I'll be along in a few minutes so we can talk about what we should do next."

"What are you going to do now?"

"Take a look upstairs in the major's room and Mr. Meadows's room."

"All right. Just a minute." Tod went to the door and looked out. "All clear," he reported. "I think the doctor's up there, but I see no sign of the other two. Don't be long."

I ran up the stairs. The room on the left was empty, but the one across the hall was obviously in use. I slipped inside. It was plain but comfortable with a carpeted floor and flowered wallpaper— much like the room we had stayed in. A curtain across one end of the room suggested a cupboard, but it turned out to be only a tier of shelves for bedding and towels. A suit of clothes hung on an open rack.

A quick glance failed to disclose anything suspicious. But then I noticed a space between the bed and the far wall. A space large enough to conceal a box. In a moment I was across the room. And there it was.

It was a wooden, iron-bound box. The bands and reinforced corners were red with rust. Earth clung to the sides and stained the scratched surface. It was *the* box. It had to be.

I opened it. It was empty.

I sat on the bed, suddenly weak-kneed. Our suspicions were confirmed. Mr. Meadows and the major had the money. But now what? What could I do about it? How could I convince anyone in the few hours I had left that those two men were guilty and my father was innocent? At that moment I heard the door close below, and then footsteps on the stairs.

I sprang to my feet and looked around in panic. There was simply no place to hide if someone came into the room. The curtain over the shelves would never conceal me, and the bed was too low to squeeze underneath. I was trapped.

I stood there, paralysed, thinking of Mr. Bowley with the knife in his chest, and the colonel lying dead in the blockhouse. The door opened. Then I sighed with relief.

It was Doctor Farr with his little black bag. He looked at me in astonishment.

"Will Martin! What are you doing here?"

"I'm looking for Mr. Meadows," I managed.

"Well, you're looking in the wrong place. This is *my* room."

It took a moment for the significance of what he said to sink in.

"*Your* room!" I looked at him in bewilderment. Then my eyes turned inevitably to the empty box. Suddenly, I remembered those bulging saddlebags on the doctor's horse. And I knew.

"*Your* room," I repeated faintly. "Then this is *your* box!"

"Yes. This is my room. And my box." The doctor looked at me for a moment through narrowed eyes. Then he moved deliberately.

He closed the door behind him and stood with his back to it. At the same time he opened his bag. He withdrew a long, tapered knife.

"I'm sorry you found it, boy," he said. There was menace in his voice. "For your sake."

22

"What—what do you mean?" I was looking at that knife, and my knees trembled with fear. "I was looking for Mr. Meadows."

"No, you weren't," he said softly. "You can't bluff your way out of this, so save your breath. You were looking for that box and you thought George Meadows had it. Why him?"

"Because he had the parrot . . ."

"Oh, I see." The doctor smiled, a cold smile. "I took the parrot from Walker's shed, and then let it go after I heard what I wanted to hear. I guess George or the major found it. They must have brought it along with them to show Mrs. Grange."

"So you—you stole the money in the first place?"

"That's right. But my accomplice got himself drowned and the parrot flew away. If you've traced the box this far, you must have a pretty good idea of what happened. You're a deal smarter than I thought you were."

I wanted to keep him talking, to delay whatever he intended to do with that wicked-looking knife.

"The parrot was supposed to tell you where to find the money?"

"Yes. Pretty good plan, except that it didn't work. It was exasperating, I can tell you, knowing a fortune was waiting for me out there, but not knowing just *where*. I should thank your father for coming into that money when he did. Too bad for him, of course, but his conviction left me free to search without rousing suspicion."

I felt my face flush with anger, but if he noticed, he paid no attention.

"I finally had a stroke of luck. A colleague of mine from Seeleys Bay told me of a patient who owned a parrot called Auld Clootie. The only trouble was that the old fool wouldn't sell. But he told me he was going to give it away—to Captain Bowley in West Port. So I bided my time. But he was slower to ship the bird than I anticipated. When I broke into old Bowley's cabin, the parrot wasn't there. And instead of being dead drunk as he usually was, Bowley caught me in his room. I had to silence him. There was a knife on the table."

I looked at the knife in his hand now, and felt a gut-churning chill deep inside me.

"You mean—you didn't kill Captain Bowley in self-defence?"

"Of course it was self-defence. If I'd let Bowley live, people would have found out that I'd broken into his place and my reputation would have been ruined. And what's one old drunkard more or less? The parrot arrived the next day, and you, of all people, delivered it and found the body. I was quite willing for you to take the bird, as you may remember, as long as I knew where I could get my hands on it. What a shock it was to find out that you are James Martin's son. How ironic!" He laughed, then became serious. "It had still never occurred to me that you would figure out the parrot's secret."

I was only half listening. He had killed two men in cold blood, and he was caressing that long, thin blade while he was blocking the door. Without moving my head, I looked around desperately for something to defend myself with. There was only a wooden chair. Nothing else . . .

"How did you find the money so quickly?" I asked.

"Oh, that. I had a patient named Zacharias Warp. A half-crazy character who talked now and then about a devil's face. So when I got the parrot's message, I simply asked Warp where it was."

"But he wouldn't tell *me*."

"So you asked him too, did you? I had some influence over him, you see. In fact I was keeping him alive with treatments. If he didn't get them, he would die—as I reminded him. It was as simple as that. He co-operated at once. Not only did he tell me where the face was, he came along and helped me dig the box up. Then, as it turned out, he didn't get the treatment anyway."

I would have paled at that, but the blood had long since drained from my face. His callous words horrified me.

"You mean, you—you killed him too?"

"Certainly not!" He pretended to be shocked. "I just didn't keep him alive. There's a difference. Now, my young friend, what am I going to do with you?"

"You can't kill me too," I said, trying to sound convincing. "You wouldn't get away with it. People know I'm here."

"Oh, I think I would. This—" he touched his finger lightly on the point of the knife—"makes a very small puncture. And I'm the doctor. I determine the cause of death. I could think of something appropriate. But it need not come to that."

I felt a twinge of hope. "What do you mean?"

"I have a lot of money in my saddlebags. More than I need. I'm willing to share it with you. That way you can live—and in comfort. How about it?"

But I knew he couldn't mean that. As long as I was alive I would be a threat. He *had* to kill me. Perhaps he was trying to lure me around the bed that separated us.

"Look," I said desperately, "I don't care about the money. You can have it all. All I want to do is save my father's life."

"Very noble," he sneered. "But there's no way you can do that without dragging me into it. And after coming this far, I'm not about to let that happen."

He intended to kill me, of course. I had to act fast. There was only the chair. With a sudden movement, I caught it up and whirled it above my head.

I guess he thought I was coming at him. But an unwieldy chair is a poor weapon against a knife in the hands of a powerful man. Instead I swung around, smashed the chair through the window, and sprang through the shattered glass.

I had no idea what awaited me below. I just knew that anything would be better than a knife in the ribs.

To this day I don't know what I hit. I do know that I hit it hard. My knees buckled and I fell flat, striking my head.

Dazed, I struggled up and tried to run. I ran smack into the side of the house and fell again. Dizzy with pain, I just wanted to lie there and let the darkness overwhelm me. But I knew I couldn't do that. After a few seconds—it felt like hours—I was up once more.

I had to run. Into the village, I told myself. Into the village where there would be people and Doctor Farr wouldn't dare attack me. But when I rounded the corner, there he was, coming out the door. I had no choice. I turned and stumbled into the fringe of trees between the house and the lake.

Almost at once I lost my footing. I fell and rolled down the embankment to the very shore of the lake.

In front of me stretched what looked like a solid floor of logs, covering the surface of the mill pond.

I had seen lumbermen walk on floating logs, with the logs not even flinching under their weight. If those big, burly chaps could do it, surely I could too, I thought recklessly. I would simply run across the pond as if I were running across a corduroy road. I didn't realize . . .

I stepped on the first log. To my dazed surprise, it started to sink. I tried to step back to safety, but the log started to roll, pitching me forwards. I had no choice but to reach out to the next log with my foot. And the next after that.

And so began a nightmare dash across the lake. No, it was hardly a dash. More like a weird, macabre dance.

I had no idea what the doctor was doing behind me. I could only think about keeping my balance, and the only way to do that was to proceed, willy-nilly, from one sinking log to the next before the first one sank beneath me and took me with it. I had to step on each log precisely so that its roll would carry me forwards. I suppose I was halfway across when the inevitable happened.

I failed to land on the next log as I wished. It rolled backwards, stopping my headlong plunge. I tried to step back, but the log under me was sinking too fast. I did the only thing I could think of.

I fell backwards, flat on my back, spreading my weight over several logs. It worked. They held, just under the surface. I lay there with the water gently lapping about me. If Doctor Farr was still coming, I had no defence left.

For just a moment I closed my eyes, gathering my scattered wits. Then I rolled carefully onto my stomach and looked back.

Doctor Farr was coming, but I think by this time he had forgotten all about me. His only concern was to keep his balance. And at that moment he lost it.

Instead of doing what I had done, he tried desperately to remain upright. The log began to sink under him, till only his upper body was in sight. He grabbed for the next log and tried to pull himself up, but it too began to sink. Another moved in, crushing him, forcing him under. For a moment only his head was visible, mouth open in a soundless scream, then just a groping hand. Then nothing. He disappeared beneath the corduroy surface of the pond.

23

Mr. Meadows and Major Hammond rescued me by pushing planks across the surface of the logs. They had seen me fleeing from the doctor and had come running. So had Tod and Tabitha. They had seen it all from our meeting place. There was nothing to indicate that the doctor had been there. The logs had closed in around him.

"We won't find him," said the major. "Not till some of those logs are out of here. Now, young fellow, what on earth was that all about?"

I was still dazed. My head hurt and I was shaking as if I had the ague. I wished I could tell everyone to go away and leave me alone. But of course I couldn't do that. Everything that the three of us had done and endured would be wasted if I didn't act at once.

I looked at the major, the bluff army man I had wrongfully suspected of being a thief and a murderer. What a relief if I could convince *him* and leave everything in his capable hands!

"Major Hammond," I said unsteadily, "if you will go up to the doctor's room in Mrs. Grange's house, you will find there an empty box—the box that was stolen from the blockhouse when Colonel Forrester was murdered. Doctor Farr's horse is hitched to the verandah post. If you look in the saddlebags, you will find the money that was in the box. Then you will know it was Doctor Farr who stole the money and killed the colonel, and that my father had nothing to do with it. And," I added despairingly, "my father is to hang for it at dawn tomorrow."

I have to hand it to Major Hammond. He didn't waste time asking questions.

"We'll see," he said. "You wait here. I'll be right back." He turned and ran to the house.

George Meadows looked at me standing between my two friends. Tod had one of my arms linked in his and Tabitha had the other while holding the bridle of her horse. For a moment he didn't say anything. Then he shook his head in wonder.

"If what you say is right, I should apologize. I had no doubt of your father's guilt. The evidence seemed conclusive."

"In that case," I said, "I should apologize as well.

For a while, I was sure you and Major Hammond had done it."

He looked startled at that, and was about to demand an explanation, when Tabitha spoke up.

"What are we going to do? Will must get to Brockville right away if he is to save his father. He'll never get there in time by boat and stage."

"You're right," said her stepfather decisively. "It's too late for that. There's only one way. Will, do you ride?"

"Ride? A bit—"

"Then take Tabitha's horse. Ajax is a good horse and will get you there by dusk."

"Yes, take Ajax," said Tabitha eagerly. "He'll get you there."

"Thank you both," I said sadly. "But if I do get there by dusk, who's going to believe me? Even if I take the money with me, they'll claim we had it in the family all along. I have no authority—"

"Never mind," interrupted George Meadows. "Major Hammond has authority. He'll go with you. They'll listen to him, I promise you. He can take the doctor's horse, saddlebags and all. I'd go myself if it would do any good. It's the least we can do."

Tabitha was pressing Ajax's reins into my hand. "Go, Will. And God go with you. When it's all over, when you can, come back to West Port—to see Tod and me."

For a moment my feelings of affection for my two friends were overwhelming. They had stood by me. Without them I would have failed. And now I had to leave them. That hurt. But there was no choice. My task wasn't finished yet. Of course I would come back, but I couldn't say so. I couldn't speak.

I think I would have kissed Tabby if Mr. Meadows hadn't been there; but we embraced, all three of us, and then I broke away and pulled myself into the saddle.

And so in a few minutes Major Hammond and I were riding madly through the bush back to West Port, then across to Newboro, and along the Brockville road.

I grew more saddle-sore and impatient with every mile. The doctor's horse, laden with the incriminating money, held us back when I wanted to gallop, to cover the weary distance to where Sarah would be waiting out those last few hours of Father's life. She must be thinking that I had failed, maybe even that I had deserted them in their time of crisis. And Father. Had he lost faith in me? Tortured thoughts burned within me, and I tried to push them away by dreaming of the future, a future when Father would be proclaimed innocent and we could resume our former happy lives. I looked across at the reassuring figure of the major and I thanked God for him, at the same time wishing he could somehow speed things up.

Fortunately, we were able to secure fresh horses at an inn about halfway to Brockville. We arrived home when the first lamps were casting their warm glow through the windows of the Brockville houses.

"Now, Will," said the major, "you go and get your sister and bring her to the prison. I'll go ahead and talk to the governor. I can't promise anything, but I'm sure that he'll listen, and we'll at least get a stay of execution. Away you go."

Our house was in darkness. I stared at it in dismay. Where could Sarah be? I had pictured my triumphant return and Sarah's unbounded joy. And now—she wasn't even here to greet me. Could she be at the prison? I was late. I doubted if she would be permitted a visit at this hour. But maybe, since this was the last night before . . .

Then I remembered. The Campbells had wanted her to stay with them. I wheeled my mount and galloped to the house beside the big church.

Mrs. Campbell answered my anxious knock.

"Will! Thank God you're here. Sarah has given up on you. Go right on in."

She was seated at a table, her head on her arms. She looked up at me, eyes dry in a deathly white face.

For a moment she said nothing, her eyes widening, then she breathed one word.

"Will!" And the tears gushed, and she sprang up, upsetting her chair, and we were clasped in a fierce embrace.

"Oh, Will," she whispered at last, "where were you? Oh, how we missed you. You're here now, but you're too late. They let me visit Papa two hours ago. For the last time. He asked about you. I told him you were coming, that we would try to get you in to see him. But he knew I was only trying to cheer him up. I could see his heart was breaking. But we have to try . . ."

"Sarah! Listen to me. Father's innocent. I know we always knew that. But now I can prove it. I found the real murderer!"

"Oh, Will!" She stared at me, hope battling despair. For a moment I wished I hadn't said that. What if Major Hammond failed? What if the governor refused to listen to him? To have hope raised, only to have it dashed, would be devastating. But I had said it. Now I had to press on.

"What—what can you do, Will? There's no time left. Can you prove it now—tonight? Will anyone listen?"

"They must listen! I've brought an army officer with me. He has the evidence. He's gone to see the governor and he's going to arrange a meeting for us with Papa. We're to meet him at the jail. Come with me, Sarah, now."

"Yes, dear," urged Mrs. Campbell. "Go. Arthur came in from a visit not ten minutes ago, so the buggy's still hitched. He'll take you. Get your wrap and go with Will."

We rode in silence to the prison, hands tightly clasped. We both knew, in spite of my words, that time was running dangerously short, that maybe even Major Hammond would be unable to save our father before the fateful hour of dawn.

So we reached the prison. We were met at the door by someone who seemed to be expecting us, and we were ushered into the visitors room.

We sat there for I don't know how long. It seemed like an eternity—an eternity of alternating hope and despair.

Then the door opened. Father came in. He was as thin and pale as a ghost. He crossed the room unsteadily, like one in a daze. Then he stopped before Sarah and me. He reached out shaking hands to us.

"I'm free!" he whispered, unbelieving. "I'm free!"

A week later, a package was delivered to our house. It was bound up in a sheet, and was perhaps the shape and size of a human head. There was a tag attached which said, "To Will Martin. A gift from the Meadows family."

I had barely started to unwrap it when a heart-stopping screech shattered the silence. And then a familiar voice, harsh but clear, made a pronounce-ment: "Trust in the Lord and don't despair."

I tore the sheet off and there it was, the gorgeous "talking feather duster," all green and gold and scarlet feathers.

"Auld Clootie knows," it said, winking black eyes at me. "Auld Clootie knows."